OTHER LIVES

OTHER LIVES

by Iman Humaydan

translated by Michelle Hartman

Interlink Books

An imprint of Interlink Publishing Group, Inc.
Northampton, Massachusetts

First published in 2014 by
INTERLINK BOOKS
An imprint of Interlink Publishing Group, Inc.
46 Crosby Street, Northampton, Massachusetts 01060
www.interlinkbooks.com

Library of Congress Cataloging-in-Publication Data
Humaydan, Iman.
[Hayawat ukhrá. English]
Other lives / by Iman Humaydan ; translated by Michelle Hartman.
    pages cm
ISBN 978-1-56656-962-0
I. Hartman, Michelle, translator. II. Title.
PJ7874.U475H3913 2014
892.7'36--dc23
                        2014002427

Printed and bound in the United States of America

To request a free copy of our 48-page full-color catalog, please call us toll-
free at 1-800-238-LINK, visit our website at www.interlinkbooks.com, or
write to us at: Interlink Publishing, 46 Crosby Street, Northampton,
Massachusetts 01060

For Inaam and May,
eternally here even though they're gone

When *will you be back home?*

He asks me on our way to the Mombasa airport. I don't say that I am coming back. I don't say that I'm leaving. I only say that I miss Lebanon. I know that longing is not for a specific place. It's for what's inside myself that I'm losing everyday, for what I lose while away, for what I've created from the images I've preserved in my head for so long. It's as though nothing is left of them now… More than fifteen years have passed since I left. I know that by going back to Beirut, I won't retrieve what I've lost. Instead I'll simply confirm my loss. I'll confirm that what I've been missing is in my head, only in my head, and I won't be able to convey it to him.

I leave Chris behind. And I leave his letter to me on my bedside table, without opening it. I know what's inside: money I don't want and a question about when I'll come back to him. Since we've been married, he's left me money in envelopes. Our hands have never touched, not even once, when he's given me money.

The day before my trip from Kenya to Lebanon, Chris is busy in his laboratory when I call him. His assistant answers. I hang up so that Chris can call me back a few moments later. He's so completely taken up with what he wants to say that he doesn't even ask what I want. In an excited, anxious voice—almost crying—he informs me that he's gotten amazing results from the experiments he began a year ago. Of course he's happy with the results of his experiments. But his happiness doesn't make me forget either my decision or my anxious desire to pack and lock my suitcases and put them by the door. I open an empty suitcase and without thinking put some clothes and other things in it. I start by opening the drawers in my wardrobe, take out my underwear, cotton t-shirts and jeans. After I pile them up on the bed, I think it's too much—I should get used to traveling lighter.

I tell myself that the airplane is taking off tomorrow morning at eight, so I have to be at the airport at six. This means I have to wake up at four in the morning—it's already past midnight and I haven't slept yet. I'm going to travel first from Mombasa to Nairobi. I don't know how long I'll have to wait in the airport there until the plane carries me to Dubai and then to Lebanon. Chris will accompany me on my journey as far as the Nairobi airport. Then he'll come back to Mombasa where our house and his work are. I won't miss anything. This is what I tell myself when I visit the rooms of the house where I've lived for eleven years and haven't left except for a quick trip to Adelaide every year, where my unbalanced father, Salama, and my silent mother, Nadia, live. Or for a short break to South Africa. I don't leave him except for intermittent weekend trips. I used to travel from Mombasa to Nairobi to pick up things that Olga sent me from Beirut. The English-language lessons dedicated to eradicating illiteracy that I used to give at UNICEF schools in Mombasa were not enough to fill periods of time as vast as the Kenyan plains, nor were the private Arabic lessons I used to teach. I've never gotten to know Kenya, despite going as a tourist on organized trips through the Kenyan mountains, the surrounding savannahs and to its parks and wildlife reserves.

Beirut… How faraway it is now. How many lives have I lived since I left it? I think while closing my second suitcase, pulling it toward the door of the house to leave it there. Did I live many lives or only one life that was enough for many women?

Questions I don't know how to answer. I'm aware that it didn't take me long to realize that ever since I left Beirut my life changed. As soon as I arrived in Australia with my incomplete family, everything changed—even the names of holidays and when they fall. The Christmas holiday changed into the summer holiday in Adelaide, the Australian city where I lived for four years before I got married and moved to Kenya. The date of winter's arrival changed. Winter started coming in July.

We wouldn't have chosen Adelaide, except that my mother's brother Yusuf lived there. He left Lebanon before the civil war started. He was an active member of the Syrian Nationalist Party and participated in the coup of 1961, fleeing before the Lebanese army could put him in prison. An Australian man whom he met when he was training at the Tiro, the shooting range near the airport, helped him flee. He arranged travel for him first to Cyprus and from there on to Australia. I was five years old at the time. But I feel as though I can still remember my mother Nadia's fear and worry about her only brother. Perhaps this was the first shock she ever had, long before my brother Baha''s death, when she received the false report of her brother Yusuf's arrest and liquidation. That was before she learned the truth about his rescue and escape from the country.

Nadia remembers the past in relation to the incidents that marked our lifetimes. She tells me that I was born on the day of the tripartite military aggression against Abdel Nasser's Egypt in 1956 and that she was terrified of losing me while I was still a fetus in her belly on the day of the earthquake in Lebanon which cracked open many houses in the village, including her parents' house in Hasbaya. She says that my brother Baha' was born after the events of 1958 in Lebanon, when my father was in prison. She also says that my uncle Yusuf, her brother, left the country to travel abroad a few days after the coup of 1961. Nadia's no different than my grandmother Nahil, my father's mother, who sees dates of public importance in the family tree before she sees the names of individuals, to say nothing of the fact that her memory would recall any event in history before it would come up with my date of birth… or even that of Salama, i.e., my father. It's as though the individual in my family has no story unless the beginning of her or his life can be associated with an important date in history. I've often believed that our destinies are linked to these dates that describe our lives, the link mysterious, hard to untangle or reveal.

I don't know if what I remember of my uncle Yusuf is what I saw and experienced myself or if the stories about him that his sister Nadia, my mother, told made me invent a memory that grew up with me and never left. I believe that I remember the day my uncle was arrested but my grandmother Nahil tells me that I was very little and it's impossible that I could remember. She tells me that I hadn't even completed my fifth year of life yet. Despite this, whenever I think about my uncle, I can imagine how angry he must've been the night before the coup—how he would've cursed the government and the state, denouncing so many of its members as traitors.

My uncle Yusuf arrived in Australia and lived in Paradise, one of the small suburbs of Adelaide. I found the name interesting after I learned that the largest cemetery and the first crematorium in the area were located near it. This is also where the Druze who immigrated to Australia built their first cemetery. Perhaps they chose this suburb for its name, which to them means that paradise is always found on earth. Or that it's a dream deferred, equidistant between earth and heaven.

We had to live in my uncle's house when we arrived at the beginning of 1980. I hadn't seen my uncle since I was a small child. He seemed like any Anglo-Saxon who'd been born and raised in Australia, especially with the broad Australian accent that he'd adopted soon after marrying an Australian woman who worked in an office for immigrants and refugees. He'd bought a house in Adelaide and didn't move from one place to another like most of the Lebanese who arrived on the continent before and during the war.

When we emerged into the arrivals hall at the Adelaide airport, my uncle ran toward us, hugging my mother for a long time and crying while he asked her how she was. She said a few incomprehensible words, also choking on her tears. He started reminding her of things that she seemed to have forgotten or things whose details may have been buried under the weight of other memories that forced her to be silent. My mother loosened the knot around her silence while hugging my uncle, murmuring a few words, her eyes filling with tears. She began talking and spoke for a few minutes and then returned to the silence that she'd chosen from the moment of my brother's death. From then on, from the time of our arrival in Australia, it seemed that her silence began to wear her out—as though what she'd chosen for herself began to exhaust her.

Everything that she'd said about Yusuf is still true. Even though he knew the story of how she fell silent after my brother Baha''s murder, he was not surprised at her words. But her words surprised me, like summer rain. They revived me and helped me recover from the wearying journey that lasted more than two days. I didn't care what she'd said about my uncle Yusuf, my only concern was that she had spoken after her long silence. In the car on the way to the house, my uncle hugged her and she cried while my father looked out of the car window at people, buildings and streets. His face was red. Sweat ran down both sides of his head and neck as though he was in a sauna. He was still wearing the woolen sweater that he'd worn to travel in from Lebanon. He insisted that it was winter and wouldn't take it off even though it was so hot in Adelaide. At that moment he seemed weak and yielding, with no power or might. He stuck his head out of the car window, turning it every which way to look at buildings and people walking by as though watching a film that was whizzing past him. He kept repeating, like a broken record, "Ism Allah, Ism Allah, keep the Evil Eye far away."

My uncle hadn't changed, that's what my mother said. But he had really started to belong to his new country over there—from a Syrian Nationalist to an Australian no different from the Anglo-Saxons. This didn't prevent him from also being an active and influential member of the Druze association that's had many different names throughout the different stages of the life of the Druze in Australia. It was first established as the Syrian Druze Association, then after Lebanese independence it became the Lebanese-Australian Association for the Druze. After the emigration of a large number of the Druze to Australia in the 1960s, before the civil war in Lebanon, the name changed three more times. It finally became and remained the Australian Druze Association and Yusuf is now in charge of it.

We stayed in my uncle's house for a few months before we found a house to move into. We rented a house nearby, in an area with few buildings other than a number of nearly identical houses all lined up next to each other on one side of the street. We left my uncle's house carrying many things that we'd accumulated. But we'd lost some of my mother's complicity with my uncle, a complicity that had always felt alive and burning to us, all those years that we were far away from him.

We were not the only Lebanese in the neighborhood; there were many Lebanese families, especially Christians and Druze. Five Lebanese families lived on our same street. Others lived on the streets that branched off ours and it didn't take us long to meet them. Their gardens revealed that the same people had lived here for a long time. These Lebanese families cared for their gardens and grew trees that reminded them of their villages and perhaps even their homes in the Lebanese mountains.

Adelaide is a city of churches. In the neighborhood where we lived there were at least four small churches that the Christian Lebanese attended every Sunday. These people had had to immigrate again after they were first displaced from their villages in the Lebanese mountains. In the nearby neighborhoods, some of the Protestant churches where only a few people prayed had transformed into banks and coffee shops and real-estate offices and houses for people who were hippies in the sixties.

Perhaps the thing that made my father the happiest about our new house was that it was located near a Lebanese bakery that had opened just one year before we arrived in Adelaide. He would go by himself to the Awaziz Bakery on Victoria Street, which branched off our street, to buy Lebanese bread and manaqeesh covered in olive oil and zaatar. The bakery sold not just bread and manaqeesh but also various pickles, zaatar and sumac, which my mother Nadia bought to put in fattoush. After a while, we started to see other things on the bakery's shelves, like cinnamon, coffee beans and apple-scented tobacco. Sometimes, in addition to these things, the owner of the bakery stocked small Lebanese flags, made in China, to respond to his customers' longing for Lebanon.

Why'd you come back to Lebanon? Why'd you return? What can you possibly expect from this country?

Olga repeats these same questions from the moment of my return to Beirut as though she doesn't know the answer.

Is it true that her incurable illness is what made me come back to Beirut? Or was it the news from the Ministry of the Displaced about reclaiming our house? Or did I come to settle old scores with a war that broke up my family, destroyed our dreams and every kind of permanence? Did I return to search for my friend Georges, who never made it to Australia? I waited for him to join me and he disappeared. They said that he left Lebanon from the port at Jounieh, but he never arrived. Perhaps he was kidnapped. Perhaps he never left and remained in Lebanon—imprisoned, lost or murdered, his corpse buried somewhere that no one in his family can find. He never reached his destination, just like so many people who left their own places for others and never arrived. On the ship that I boarded that day for Larnaca, they said that his name was recorded in the log but that no one had seen him. They said that he bade his family farewell at home and left for the port long before the ship put to sea.

What'd you come back for? Olga repeats, and then when I don't answer, she draws me to her and hugs me, scattering kisses all over my hair, face, mouth and neck. Angry? she asks me, then repeats her question: What'd you come back for?

Olga's question takes me back to an earlier fear, one that began long before my trip from Beirut, after my brother Baha"s death, which was followed soon after by Georges' disappearance. In my first letter to Olga from Adelaide I wrote, "To kill fear, it isn't enough to move to another country and live in a new house. It's already taken root inside of us and so in order to kill it we first have to kill something inside ourselves. Perhaps we have to cut off one of our limbs. I've often thought of this as a little suicide. It's as if we are looking fearlessly right into the eyes of a wild beast, looking at it and trying to kill it. We don't know at that moment that we are killing most of what's inside ourselves. But what remains after that? What remains after we've killed the fear? Does memory remain, for example? Or does it become like a blank page? And what should we fill it with?"

Olga never wrote to me much, she preferred the telephone. She would call every Thursday. She chose the day and it became our tradition. She used to call me every Thursday and I would write to her every weekend. There was a continual conversation going on between us, each one of us participating in her own way—I through letters and she through words. Our phone conversation would stretch on too long every time; I would laugh when she'd repeat news she'd already told me, protesting that I hadn't paid enough attention the week before. She'd finish by saying, "Don't forget to answer my questions in your letter." Sometimes a week or more would pass without a phone call from her and when she would speak to me she'd tell me that the phone lines were cut, that Lebanon had become a country where people are maimed, victimized, murdered, slaughtered. She'd tell me that things there were shitty and that for her things were shitty beyond shitty.

"Last time we spoke, you didn't tell me you were coming so soon…!" Olga comments. She's harassed me with this same comment since I arrived in Beirut. It's as though she doubts everything I say and doesn't believe I've returned simply to reclaim the house in Zuqaq al-Blat. I don't tell Olga that I've read her doctor's report and his description of a treatment that she rejected. I've also seen the test analyses and results.

I've collected no fewer than thirteen suitcases during my scattered migrations between Lebanon, Australia and Kenya. I put what I need in these suitcases. I still don't understand why a person would need to empty her suitcases. My suitcase has become my home. I've become a suitcase expert—special suitcases for backache, others that hold a lot though they weigh very little. I've had to find extra space in my house to put the suitcases, safe places I can get to easily when I need to.

"*What a surrealistic life!*" My English husband Chris mounts a reserved protest as he counts the suitcases piled one on top of the other.

"*How many lives do you need to fill all those?*" he asks, adding yet another comment: that I should be reincarnated and live other lives in order to fill all these suitcases. According to him, I do nothing in Mombasa except "try to find a permanent location to store my travel apparatus." This is how he describes my suitcases, trying to make a joke. When we first knew each other, his sarcastic comments would make me stop and think. I used to believe that there was poetry in his remarks and that he needed great powers of imagination to create these sentences. But with time, I'm no longer interested in these kinds of comments. I no longer laugh at his jokes; instead they make me angry. I now believe that he's so sarcastic because he can't understand that I can only calm my fears and ease my time in Mombasa by creating stable, settled places within this kind of temporary residence and deferred departure. I've started putting in *ear plugs*, those little wax balls wrapped in cotton, when he talks nonstop about his research and other ideas. I nod my head, agreeing with what he's saying as if I'm listening. I see him talking on and on, gesturing with his fingers, hands and arms. He looks like one of those sign-language interpreters on the six o'clock TV news broadcast. When he makes a circular motion with his fingers that means that everything's going as he wants it to, I don't really understand him. I laugh and doze off. No doubt I doze off while laughing.

My life feels like interrupted sequences of time, like scenes in a film that begin just as another scene ends. My memory of everything that has happened is not continuous, but circular. I always come back to where I began. When I tell my doctor this, he tries to reassure me, saying that circular memory is a peculiarity of women and that men remember differently. But I don't find this answer logical. I mix up the relationship between events and places. I'll be thinking about the day we left Beirut and then find myself suddenly jumping to the years that I've spent with Chris in Kenya. Perhaps this is why my story now takes on a circular and sometimes spiral form.

I live in Adelaide for four years that pass like the taste of the wind. I stay eleven years in Mombasa, always on the verge of leaving. "On the verge"—this expression perfectly summarizes a life scattered between Australia and Kenya. I'm like someone waiting to get out but who, at the very same time, isn't even inside. Between inside and outside, I live a suspended life, like someone waiting in a purgatory with locked doors, no bridge, no way out. I remember what Mary Douglas, the anthropologist and scholar, said in a book I read in Australia when I was trying to finish my Masters thesis. She described the state of being in-between, or "in-betweenness." She said that people pass through this stage and move into another one, which is clearer, when their lives and relationships become more regulated. My situation in no way resembles Douglas's description. For me, "in-betweenness" is a permanent way of life that will never change or be transformed into any other state.

I am going to Beirut, then.

In the Dubai airport, I pass my time in a bar on the first floor. I choose it because it has large sofas that allow me to stretch out and relax. I have to wait six hours for the plane to take me to Beirut. I have to wait what seems like a whole night. Time passes in a strange way here. I don't feel like it's nighttime, nor do I fall asleep. The place seems like a giant space station stuffed full of jewelry, toys, gifts and food. A world full of light that never sleeps. A place that I imagine withers and dies when people leave it, as if it's an imaginary world that doesn't exist. As if it's on television. The music of the whole world plays here all at once. Filipinos and Indians and Sri Lankans and Europeans and Americans. People from every country in the world walk through this airport's halls. The place lives off of them; they illuminate it. But emptiness consumes its heart, just as the desert sand consumes buildings and transforms them into skeletons that age at the speed of light.

The man in his fifties who sits on the other end of this sofa is turning the pages of an English newspaper and when I'm about to sit down he adjusts how he's sitting, closing and folding the newspaper as if offering me more space. I don't need more space; the pages of the newspaper don't hinder my movements. I put my suitcase on the seat across from me, my book and papers on the table. He starts gathering up his stuff as though getting himself ready for a trip he's unprepared for. He seems puzzled and concerned with knowing the identity of this woman who's sitting near him—that is to say, me—so he raises his head after a few minutes and, smiling, asks me in English, "*Traveling to Beirut?*"

I nod in response to his trivial question, glancing at him to be sure that this voice was his. He adds, smiling, that he's a sorcerer and in touch with the supernatural. His smile broadens as he looks at then nods toward my passport on the table in front of me, with my Middle East Airlines ticket sticking out of it. An unimpressive attempt at seduction, I say to myself wearily. I need a better, more powerful seduction to conjure up a passion I haven't lived for a long time. Despite this, a flood of feelings, like what children feel when they rush off to play with a new toy, sweeps me away. Feelings of fear and excitement together. I can smell his cologne from this distance. Perhaps it's the scent of his skin. When he stands up and comes closer, he seems cleaner and livelier than a traveler usually can be.

"*My name is Nour.*"

He says to me in English, extending his arm out in front of him as though to shake my hand. Nour... I smile. I didn't expect him to have an Arabic name with his American accent. He's wearing jeans and a blue shirt with thin white stripes. He acts as though he's spent a long time preparing for the excursion to come over and introduce himself to me. He asks if he can share my hot chocolate and then gently places my leather suitcase beside me so that he can sit down across from me before I've even answered.

I don't know how much time passes before I look him in the eyes. Without extending my hand, I say in English, slowly and neutrally, "*I am Myriam.*"

Slow and neutral, I think, while sipping hot chocolate, which burns my tongue and the roof of my mouth… "Slowly and neutrally." I keep reminding myself that since leaving Beirut my behavior has been formed by a selection of well-learned techniques that I use to connect or not to connect to people. He tells me that he's lived in America since he was ten years old and that he left it for Lebanon this year. He was visiting Dubai for just a week for his work as a journalist and now is returning to Lebanon because he was born there and wants to get to know the country that he hasn't visited since 1967. He's returning to search for his roots. It's amusing to me that when talking about his roots, repeating the same sentence many times, he curls his lips and raises his voice higher and sharper than before:

"*I'm searching for my roots!*"

Nour's father is Palestinian, he has a Lebanese mother, but he doesn't speak Arabic. He doesn't know his mother tongue, I say to myself. I have to make a huge effort to listen to him and respond to his questions, just as I do with Chris. In a few moments that feel like a very long time, he tells me about his family, his life and his American wife and daughter. It seems as though this life of his fatigues him and, using rapid, exuberant words, he wants to hand it over for safekeeping to the first person who'll listen to him. By chance, I am that person. A woman he just met in an airport. I think, I don't have space for other people's lives, my own life's enough for me. It's enough that I'm continually attempting to gather my life together, given my overwhelming suspicion that I lack the proper tools.

When faced with these thoughts, my body grows restless and I suddenly feel like a combatant preparing for an attack. At that moment, I feel unable to gather myself in one place and one memory; his speech confuses me and makes me more anxious. But I hear myself saying to him, with open sarcasm, "*Why bother searching for roots, I can give you as much as you want, a surplus I want to get rid of!*"

Why bother to search? I can give you all you want, I have a surplus of roots and I want to be done with them! He wasn't expecting such an answer. And I don't think about what I'm saying before this sentence pops out of my mouth. Perhaps it came from a confused, impotent thought that has grown and been nurtured by the travels I've been forced to make between Lebanon, Australia and Africa; roots are something that we ourselves re-fabricate and completely modify, just as when we prepare food, we add spices according to our tastes. During the conversation a quick, tense understanding develops naturally between us, from the sentences we exchange and the thin, friendly laughter we generate.

He was born in 1945 in Lebanon and was a boy when he immigrated with his parents to the United States. He returned after their death to get to know his mother's country. In Beirut he rents a small apartment paid for by the American newspaper for which he's a correspondent. I cannot go back to Palestine, of course, Nour continues, they destroyed my paternal grandfather's house there 30 years ago. He used to visit this house in Palestine until 1967, when he could no longer enter. He says that he's forgotten nearly everything and only remembers the smells of the food, which he feels are always there, nearby. He came back searching for these smells. In America, he cooks for himself and his American friends, whom he invites over to hang out at his house on Saturday nights. He prepares recipes that he learned from his mother and he has many cookbooks from which he's learned Palestinian and Lebanese recipes.

He tells the story of his family chronologically, as though reading it from a book, as though his memories have no pain attached to them. My memories always spiral when I narrate them. I begin with a story and find myself returning to it. He narrates exotically, as though I myself were foreign to him and he needs to make sure the story follows a chronological progression in order for me to understand it. On the plane, Nour tells me the story of his life. He has a deep need to tell me everything about himself. Intimate conversations are easier when we're moving from one place to another. Perhaps because he's in such a state, his words are quickly left behind—they aren't a heavy burden weighing us down.

On the plane I learn to surrender to my fear to remain relaxed and calm, in total surrender to the possibility of death, to a fear that could swallow me up and not terrify me.

I lean my head against the glass of the airplane's small window while Nour, who manages to get seated next to me, starts reading a book that he took out of his small suitcase. Its author, Elia Kazan, put much of his life story in it, the story of his Turkish, Greek, Armenian family, the story of their immigration to the United States and a discussion of identity and assimilation. I read the title on its cover: *The Arrangement*.

Nour opens to a page and starts reading, aloud, a part of the novel in which an old man, nearing death, asks for grapes from Smyrna, or Izmir, grapes that he hasn't been able to eat since he emigrated from Anatolia. After a long life's journey, changes, forgetting, adaptation and making a new life—after all this, it seems the only desire left in the father's memory is for grapes from Smyrna. Nour's reading penetrates me, his words flow deeply inside of me while I'm somewhere between sleeping and waking on the airplane, trying desperately to remain awake so I can listen to him.

When his words enter my head, they transform into colorful pictures coming from a memory behind forgetfulness—pictures from the day my uncle traveled abroad and from the day we left. His words transform into questions, born of stories told about my family's emigration. What does our emigration mean, what does it mean to belong to another country and another civilization? We emigrate and build another life and believe that we've been saved. But at a certain moment, everything that we have built becomes ruined and we return to a past that we reckoned had disappeared or that we had intentionally forgotten, throwing it somewhere under thick layers of memory.

Idea after idea bores into my head, entering with Nour's voice; it's difficult to know if I'm asleep and having these thoughts like dreams or awake and talking to myself. There's no doubt that I've nodded off. I'm warm and happy like a small kitten, especially since for once I don't have a headache. A chronic pain emigrated with me from Beirut fifteen years ago and has never left.

I wake up in the airplane and a warm feeling of contentment floods through me when I find myself wrapped in the blue woolen blanket that Nour pulled over me while I was sleeping. I take two migraine pills. I started taking them not long before my trip from Lebanon. My medicine is my constant companion; I take it before I even feel the pain. I take it to be sure the pain will not suddenly seize me.

When he asks why I'm returning to Lebanon I tell him that it's not a "return," but that I'm coming to reclaim a house that I thought I'd lost. I don't know why I keep insisting that my return is temporary, that I'm not remaining in Beirut. Do I insist on this to this man whom I hardly know because I fear the passion with which he speaks about his own return? About the Lebanon that he began to rediscover only a year ago? About the place of his father's birth in Palestine and his family and childhood stories from Lebanon, his mother's country? I tell him that my stay in Beirut is temporary and that I'll return home soon. I repeat this to him, perhaps more to convince myself that nothing could change my decision to return to Africa.

Nour returns to search for his roots. As a journalist he may decide where he wants to travel and he's chosen Lebanon, the country where he spent his childhood before he left for America. As for me, I've come to sell the building that I inherited from my parents, then return to

Kenya. I'll be able to sell it only after the displaced people living in it are evicted. I only inherited it because my brother Baha' was killed. Of course my brother would have been first in line to inherit the house, he was the only man in the family, just like my father Salama before him when he inherited the house from my grandfather Hamza. Baha' was killed in the beginning of 1978, almost three years after the civil war started in Lebanon. He died when a rocket explosion sent shrapnel flying onto the balcony of the second floor of our house in Zuqaq al-Blat, where he stood. We couldn't recognize him. They brought a coffin and told our family, "Your son's inside." Two days after the burial, young men from the neighborhood found pieces of his limbs hanging from the branches of the few trees that were not also burned in the explosion. The smell of my brother's burning body remains in the house for a long time. Sometimes I feel as though this smell is still close to me, that since the incident my senses can no longer perceive any other smell. My father was also injured that day, with a head wound. He recovered, but a short time later he started acting strangely. The doctor doesn't want to remove the piece of shrapnel from his head because of the danger of injuring him further. And as for my mother, she stopped speaking all together. The shock of my brother's death made her lose the power of speech. When she wants to say something she gestures with her fingers, drawing empty circles in the air. This is how we leave Lebanon for Adelaide, where my uncle went when he emigrated many years before the war. We leave: my incomplete, amputated family made up of an almost insane father, a mother who refuses to speak, and a daughter who is waiting for a man to follow her to Australia, a man whom she'll never see again after she leaves.

We leave Lebanon for Adelaide two years after my brother Baha"'s death and my grandmother Nahil's failed attempts to get my father to have another son by a younger wife. My uncle Yusuf comes up with the idea of immigration in a letter. He tells us that staying in Lebanon is a slow suicide and that my mother's silence and my father's madness are both signs of this. The day we leave, my sick father still thinks that his mother Nahil will be traveling with us to Australia. Even though she's told him, "Here and there are just the same, why would I travel?" following up with, "Every country on earth is just the same, everywhere you go, all people are the same too." When we leave, she doesn't wait at the door like someone who has come to see people off; she doesn't cry in front of us. Rather, she turns her back after saying goodbye to my father and goes into her room, locking the door behind her. To someone from the outside looking at her, she might appear angry at her son Salama. Angry that he's failed to take care of us, angry that his second marriage, which she arranged for him, has failed, that he's failed to have another son who could take Baha"'s place. Angry that the family is splitting apart despite her belief in her efforts to plan its future. But I know that there are sure to be tears in her eyes at the moment of farewell. I know that after she locks the door behind her she takes out the Hikmeh, which she keeps with meticulous care in her closet, and opens it, letting the pages fall open at random and reading whatever passage it opens to. She reads, peering into the words transcribed in front of her in a wide, black, zigzagging handwriting, and seeks a full future for the family. Only at that moment would Nahil's faith return to her and her anger pass. She'd stop doubting that the future the book shows her would be realized. It's as though for her the future were a film playing over and over, its scenes seeming more natural each time.

My grandmother Nahil won't agree to leave with us, just as in the past she wouldn't agree to leave her house in the mountains and come with my grandfather Hamza to live in Beirut after he bought the Turkish Damad family's building in Zuqaq al-Blat. This is likely because she believed that my grandfather Hamza would no longer put effort into his work or business after buying this two-story building. "The threshold to this house is ill-fated," she used to always repeat, adding, "Nothing pure nor good can come from nourishment you've taken from your friend's mouth by deceit." Nahil's convictions and fears, however, didn't stop Hamza from renovating the old building, adding new rooms on the second floor, which had consisted of just two small rooms and an empty roof. He decorated the high walls and new door frames with calligraphy carved by masons who came from the mountains especially for this work. He added carvings of gilded letters, in green and yellow, blue and red, placing them on top of the five gates of the house. Nahil's resistance didn't last long. She left the house in the mountains when Hamza finished renovating the house in

Zuqaq al-Blat. She wouldn't return to the mountains at all until after he died.

My grandfather tries in every way he can to suggest that the house is his, that he'd inherited it from relatives about whom we know nothing. Perhaps all the changes he makes to the house are an effort to erase the story of its family and his own story too. How he came as a child from Syria with his impoverished parents and worked in construction on the train station in Sofar. He then worked as a driver for the Turkish Damad family, who showered him with money and assistance so that afterward he became a businessman, selling bread and drinks and ice to passengers on the Beirut–Damascus train line, which passed through the Sofar station. How he bought the house cheap from the Damad widow after her husband's accidental death in the Gallata fire in Istanbul that destroyed everything the man owned. She needed money to emigrate to America, following her family who was already there, so she sold her house cheap—for the price of dirt, my grandmother Nahil used to say. My grandfather Hamza, though, told a completely different story. He would always say that he bought the house as a favor to the Turkish man's widow. He'd say that he would've rather bought land in his village that was covered with profitable olive trees, but instead bought a modest, ramshackle old house with hardly any land around it, except a small lot filled with prickly pear cactus. People in the village made fun of him and said that he'd lost his mind. He'd claim that he chose to buy the house as a favor to a man who helped him and died leaving behind a wife with no money who wanted to emigrate and join her family in America.

In Kenya, I always dream that I'm in Lebanon, in the house that I've left. I wake up many times in the night and I fall back to sleep every time to the sounds of Indian Ocean. The waves almost reach my always-damp garden, then recede in a never-ending play of ebb and flow.

Sometimes I leave my bedroom and go into the garden when the moon is full and I don't need anything to light my path. The light of the moon shines on the ever so slowly receding water and I quickly fall asleep. I fall asleep on the sand or on the straw chair at the bottom of the garden near the walls made of the trunks of coconut trees.

I've always lived my dreams there as though they were a part of my life. They accompany me in the daylight hours and I don't forget them. I wake up in the morning and think about what I was dreaming the night before. When I tell Eva, my Austrian neighbor and only friend in Mombasa, about what seemed to be my only dream, she tells me not to be scared. She tells me that the skies of Kenya are vast and that dreams, however many you have, evaporate in the sky.

Perhaps I should call my dreams nightmares. I remember the explosion that murdered my brother Baha' in Beirut. From that time on God stopped visiting me in my dreams. Perhaps that was the moment when my dreams became nightmares. We wanted to go down to the shelter that day, but my mother Nadia insisted on staying on the second floor. She usually didn't insist on anything, but that day she did. She usually lived the fairly submissive life that Nahil wanted—because my grandmother controlled her life just as she controlled the house and our lives—detached from her own desires. Nadia lived submissively. And then when she finally asserted an opinion, she was immediately silenced! She went silent both out of shock and as a protest. Her silence angers me just as the submissiveness she showed to my father Salama's family angered me in the past. She didn't want to go down into the shelter and insisted that we all stay together on the first floor. It was as if, on that one day, she wanted to avenge her life. But instead she lost my brother Baha'.

On the night before my trip from Mombasa to Beirut, Chris comes to me filled with desire and kisses my face and neck. He runs his hand over the breasts he loves and with his other arm tries to pull my body close to him, repeating, Oh Myriam, love me, love me please.

I feel utterly weak, almost paralyzed, when we are in bed and Chris starts talking. To overcome this paralysis, I resort to a fantasy that gives me pleasure. Over time, I've grown used to this thing that happens between us: him approaching me and letting his hand discover my body anew. I'm also used to putting my fantasies to work as soon as he starts kissing me, stripping off my clothes and repeating words under his breath that increase his desire. I let myself be free and move my body to the rhythm of Asmahan's voice coming from the corner of the room. I begin a game of the body, separate from the memory of true love. In the absence of the man I love, I think that I will surely adapt to the situation that I myself consented to when I left Beirut. I let myself share pleasure with a man whom I don't love even though he is filled with desire and tries to please me.

When he starts flirting with me I always fantasize that he is Georges, or Joe, the man I met in an Italian restaurant in South Africa. I carried on a brief affair with Joe; it only lasted a year, during which I visited Cape Town seven times to meet him in some random hotel room. My Austrian friend Eva used to leave deliberately when the phone would ring for me in the hotel room, telling me before she shut the door behind her that we didn't have much time—she just has to go back to the market once more. She'd hug me, leaving her arms around my body for a long time as though she feared losing me, mumbling words from which I understand that she can't say anything. Then she'd walk backward, looking at me the whole time and leave. Eva only hugged me like this when she knew that I had a rendezvous with Joe. A hug with an equal mix of love and reproach that's hard to explain: it's like the hug of a mother who's just discovered that her daughter has given her virginity to the neighbor's son. Lying on the bed, I watched Eva close the door of the hotel room on me. I don't know why at that moment an idea powerfully overtook me—that betrayal is a defense against the absence of love. Joe also came to Mombasa to meet me at the Gardens Hotel. After a year, I decided to stop seeing him. When he asked me why, I didn't know what to answer. I searched for just one word to tell him and I couldn't find it. I've grown tired. I'm tired of traveling. I'm tired of the repetition, of the heaviness of a sick, disabled relationship that can't develop.

"The animal in you is tired of you..." Eva says when I end my relationship with Joe, poetic as usual, sometimes she's even musical. I consider how Eva could become a famous poet, though she prefers to be an environmental activist working with endangered animals and sick trees and forests.

Sometimes I leave my fantasies and remember specific moments in my life, like when I first discovered my body with Olga. We'd leave Asmahan's voice playing and Olga would start kissing me on my mouth and breasts. I try hard to recall the moments of happiness that we lived together—Olga and I—without feeling I was doing something wrong. But that one night with Chris I can't get my fantasies working. It's as though I'm afflicted by a loss of memory or my fantasies can no longer help me tune into Georges or Joe's features. The faces of everyone with whom I've shared pleasure suddenly vanish, as if they've all passed through my life quickly, in one stroke of forgetfulness. As if they never were. I try to recall their features but their faces are nebulous and unclear, their eyes all distorted and staring at me standing right in front of them. An invisible force is pushing them back. I try to recall Olga's face and I see it vividly, as if it were right there in front of me. I turn my gaze away, toward my suitcase, and start recounting the previous night's dream to Chris. I dream I'm a tree, a very tall tree, swaying in the breeze. I tell him that in the dream I'm a tree. He's far away from me and can't touch me. And I'm feeling a strange kind of pleasure, as though the wind itself were making love to me. I know that I reach orgasm but I don't know how. It's enough to hear the tree's leaves rustle in the gentle breeze to feel an excitement that no man can arouse in me.

It's not Asmahan's voice alone that transports me to this memory that I love and that helps me bear my life in Kenya. There are also the novels that Olga sends me and the vivid colors of the sky reflected in sea surrounding my house—bright colors, more vivid than the sky's colors in Beirut and more brilliant.

My dreams change and I forget most of them, except those that repeat themselves and invade me, year after year. There are many trees and plants and mountains in them that I'm always able to fly above easily. When I try to fall sleep I recall those dreams. As if I choose my dreams to push away the nightmare that's lived with me for so many years. My dream of friendly trees is perhaps some kind of recompense. After my brother Baha"s death, I so often see burning trees with the disfigured faces of featureless people hovering above them. I begin to fear trees. I no longer dream that I'm walking above them, as if walking on the ground. I no longer dream that I'm flying above them, never landing. Trees themselves become pure terror.

Sometimes I wake up afraid, then my headache worsens and I don't know if it's the pain or my nightmares that have awoken me. I leave the bedroom on my tiptoes, open the door that faces the Indian Ocean in Mombasa and go out into the garden. I sit on the white sand that reflects the moonlight with incandescent, silvery colors. Silver stretches out over the surface of the sand and together they enter the depths of the water in the distance. The water mingles with the nighttime light from a distance like an incomplete rainbow. The sounds of the waves recur in a rhythm like sex between two lovers who never get bored. I am quickly overcome and fall asleep on the sand, only to wake up with water flowing around me on all sides. Nothing eases my severe headaches except the play of the sea, its ebb and flow, its humidity and saltiness. The sea is absorbed by the sand and submerges me like an act of total love. The most beautiful thing I experienced living in Mombasa was my discovery of the sea's playful ebb and flow. This calms my anxiety as though taming it. Ebb and flow, like the play between dreams and nightmares, my life here and my life there, the silence of my mother and the madness of my father. Ebb and flow... past and present. Whenever I think I have forgotten the past, it forces itself on me again in all my dreams.

There's no distance at all between ebb and flow in my psychoanalyst Seetajeet's clinic in Mombasa. They mix and mingle completely and I can no longer distinguish between them. This is not what exhausts me, though. What exhausts me is speaking in a language that is not my own about things that pain me, that make me cry. I must to talk to a British doctor of Indian origin in a language that is not my own. In these moments I feel like someone digging an enormous hole with only one soft, weak hand. I want him to understand and to help me understand myself, what's happening to me. I want him to help me be delivered from sins I have not committed: the sin of my brother's death, the sin of my mother's silence, the sin of my father's madness... the sin of being forced to abort my baby, the baby that I'm not yet able to conceive with Chris, as though I am being punished. But for three years I haven't been sure if my psychoanalyst understands me. Sometimes he comments on what I've said at moments when I really want him to stay silent. I don't know how to speak another language and cry at the same time. But I don't stop seeing him, either. I start speaking English with an Indian accent to be sure that what I'm saying is clear and understandable. Sometimes I find myself speaking Arabic inadvertently. When I notice, I suddenly fall silent, as if I've lost my voice. There is a painful quality to this silence. It takes some time to get back to my second or third language. Languages collide in my head and prevent words from escaping from my mouth. The Arabic language no longer emerges clearly; it's weepy and convulsive. I raise my head from the pillow on the couch and look at him suddenly, only to find his eyes closed, as though he's been taken by a passing distraction. Or perhaps he didn't notice what was happening, didn't notice my words in Arabic, words he can't understand.

Look at me, I say to him choking on my tears, *Look at me! You are not with me...!*

He doesn't respond. He opens his eyes, looking straight ahead, far away from me, and not meeting my gaze.

"I got rid of my baby like a little bug. Now I want to get pregnant and I can't…!" I whisper in a voice emerging from deep inside me, trying to stand up at the end of the session and forgetting that the person in front of me doesn't understand the language of my skin.

I collapse on the chair and drown in a torrent of tears.

Before the plane takes off, Chris and I have a coffee together for the last time in the small building that is the Nairobi airport. The coffee is thick and I feel nauseated. The airport looks like debris from the surrounding buildings, or just broken, nothing in it working. Even the few airport employees sitting around appear to be just visiting a place where they don't understand how things work. All it takes is a glance at the windows, where flimsy nylon bags have replaced broken glass, to remember that this vast country has lived through continuous but interrupted wars, not so different than our wars. In different countries little wars have a tragic resemblance, I think, not paying attention to Chris's repeated questions. *"When are you coming back home?"*

"When are you coming back home?" he reiterates and then, when he's lost hope of me responding, "Are you coming back home?" I don't speak since I can't find a way to answer these two questions at the same time. I think about what he says, *"coming back home."* I think that we— Chris and I—simply don't see eye to eye on anything, not even on the meaning of words. For me, "coming back home" is exactly what I'm doing right now. I reflect that perhaps I'm overcome by a desire to live life, while this man spends his time dissecting that same desire. Like any serious, systematic scientist he remains at a measured distance from life in order to dissect it.

I remember the first time I arrived in Kenya from Australia. I found Chris waiting for me at the airport in Nairobi. I was scared. It was the first time I'd been in a place where I could see only black-skinned people. All of them Africans. I asked myself at that moment why I was scared. Was my fear derived from a collective memory I carry inside me, a memory of my ancestors' theft of these people's wealth—their mines and their natural resources? Was I scared of having to settle the accounts of those who came before me, whatever their nationality... those people who came, exploited them, got rich and never paid a price for anything?

Those first faces I saw remain in my mind. I've never forgotten even one of the people I saw at that moment of my arrival in the airport. I've remembered them for years. Whenever I travel, I search for them. Sometimes I spot one of them and find that he's gotten a bit older, his eyes grown hard. I recall these people when Chris is on top of me. I close my eyes and think about them. I imagine Samuel, the man who works in the garden of my house. I picture his face and his shining black skin, while Chris, after reaching orgasm, tells me about the types of malaria that people here suffer from and the differences in malaria between one African country and another.

But why am I thinking about Chris right now? Why am I remembering the habits of his that I never really related to? Is it because I am a woman without habits? Is this why the years that I spent with him in Kenya still remain somehow outside my life—as though I didn't live them? Or is it the years themselves that are outside my life? Or is it because I am outside of any place that connects me to life? Or perhaps it all goes back to Chris being particularly systematic, his life intimately linked to the ticking of the clock. He sees his life as a system of unchanging habits, while I ... drink coffee in the morning... No, no ... actually I drink tea. I smoke... no, I don't! But yes I do, I smoke sometimes. I go for a walk every morning... no, not most mornings. I always prefer to be alone at home... alone with my novels that Olga took pains to send me all those years.

Perhaps my sole habit is tied to memory: a permanent feeling of being in a transient state since I left Lebanon. In my house in Mombasa I leave my handbag on the table in the entryway, as though I'm about to leave at any minute or only there on a short trip, visiting strangers. "Myriam, this is your house. This is your house and you are its mistress, why don't you put your things away? Why do you leave stuff scattered around like this, in suitcases?" Chris always repeats these questions impatiently, in his English accent, when he sees my things left for days in the small hallway next to the front door of the house. He looks at my address book and the leather bag where I keep the novels that I receive from Lebanon. I take them with me in the car or leave them in the front garden of the house where I often sit. But Chris's words don't diminish my feelings of alienation from him—if anything they make it worse. I'm well aware that my habit of always being on alert and nervously ready for anything is something I brought with me from wartime Beirut, from the memory of bomb shelters and needing to move from one place to another, safer one. This remains inside of me, never leaving me, throughout years of nomadic moving and wandering between Adelaide and Mombasa. I know that my anxiety has become like my shadow and long ago left its imprint on my personality.

Only Samuel the Kenyan gardener offers me some sense of security. He gives me peace of mind when he tells me that moving doesn't have to mean anything, that it's possible for a person to remain at home in his heart wherever he may be. He tells me that he feels able to live multiple lives while in the very same place. When he's somewhere else, he can feel that there's another person inside him.

Samuel approaches the chair where I'm sitting in the garden and starts flipping through the books that fill the bag lying open on the grass near my feet. Some of the books are in Arabic, so look like a puzzle to him. He leaves the books, looks at me and says that every book has a life here and a life there, where it came from. He continues, "This is how I live both inside and outside." I don't understand exactly what he means, but right away I connect what he's saying to something he once told me about his old grandfather, who left the bush half-naked and came to Mombasa to live, have a family and settle down, dressing like the foreigners who lived in the city. That time he told me that he feels I understand everything, as though I too have started to carry his memories—though I'm a stranger to this land, I live this life here and share these experiences. I have started spending more time with Samuel than with Chris, who is entranced by his little insects, painstakingly fixed on glass slides under his microscope. He says that if they multiplied enough and filled the world, they could finish off humankind.

In Kenya, as in Australia, I've started taking tranquilizers and sleeping pills, but the migraines still won't leave me. I wake up in the morning and am unable to open my eyes. I close the curtains again, banishing the morning light to the outside. Light makes my migraines worse and would keep me in bed for the whole day. The curtains of my room remain drawn and I only see the daylight in Mombasa when my pain subsides. When I feel a bit better, I go out into the garden and watch Samuel cut the grass while water gushes out of the hose, submerging his muddy feet and watering the plants and trees.

To feel better, I always need to lean my head slightly forward so that the muscles on my neck press backwards and relieve the pain a little. When I go to bed, I need to put a pillow right under my neck, to ease the pain so I can sleep. But now nothing relieves the pain. When I bend my head forward it hurts, so I lean it back and the pain only gets worse. I tilt my head to the left, then to the right; later I feel that it's so heavy I can no longer hold it up. I take two Advil. Two hours later I follow up with two Diantalvic and then before I sleep a Toradol, then a

Stilnox. I go to bed still in pain, but the pain just sleeps. It gets tired, turns over and goes to sleep, while I toss and turn in the bed.

As soon as Chris comes home, he starts gathering up all my stuff that's lying around. He tidies everything back where it belongs and says again how worried he is about me and how he wants me to be more present and at home here. He walks over to the cassette player, lowering Asmahan's voice so much that he almost strangles it. I've grown used to his running commentary and the presence of two speeds and rhythms of life in the house. His rhythm and my rhythm. My rhythm is like the music of the people whom Samuel brings every day to work in the house and in the garden for a little money, who leave in the evening always carrying food that I've shared with them. As for his rhythm... it's stable and calm. Nothing about his inner life ever changes. I only feel his presence in the house when he goes into his office and stays there until after midnight, when I'm in bed, covered with a thin blanket, novels that I've started to read but haven't finished scattered around me, Asmahan's voice filling the room, keeping me company while I sleep until morning. Of course he doesn't understand why I keep the music playing while I sleep. And he doesn't understand how I can listen to the same recording one, two, three times throughout the night. These tapes of Asmahan that I brought with me from Lebanon. Other tapes that Olga sent me. Still other hard-to-find, rare ones, most of which I bought at a place near Suq al-Hamidiyyeh when I went secretly to Damascus with Georges just before Baha' was murdered in 1978. When I sleep, sometimes I dream of Asmahan. I imagine a young woman who's twenty-six years old, dying at the height of her glory. I was about her age when I lost my brother Baha' and we decided to leave Lebanon for Australia. From the time I was young I tried to invent things she and I had in common. I'd say that we both loved singing, we both came from the mountains, we both lived through wars that changed the course of our lives, our destinies. Then I'd backtrack and say that she was different from me in many ways, the most important of which is that she didn't know fear—this adventuress had no fear, the kind of fear that's inhabited me since Baha' was killed and Georges disappeared. Indeed well before this I might almost have said that it was this fear that caused Baha''s death.

As a child, I stood on a thick white fence, on the outer wall of the house's courtyard, in front of my mother Nadia and sang, "Ya habibi, come… Follow me and see what happened to me because you're away… I'm up all night because of my love, calling your shadow. Who's like you? I'm keeping my love a secret, but my love is destroying me." My father, sitting far away from us, clapped as if I were actually Asmahan and my mother encouraged me by nodding her head. When I forgot or mispronounced words she'd mouth them to me. She'd start with just the first word of that part of the song to help me remember. Then her voice would emerge, clear and deep, as if it had never been used, and then just as quickly would fall silent once I'd recovered the rhythm I'd lost for a few moments and started singing again. Sometimes she accompanied me when I sang, her voice weaker than mine. My grandmother Nahil would come outside and see me fearlessly swaying on the edge of the wall, my mother below gazing up at me, her laughing eyes brimming with tears. Nahil whispered harsh words to scold her son Salama, as usual, chastising Nadia's laxity and her failures in raising me.

She'd say all this without looking at Nadia, ignoring her presence beside me. Nahil took me down from the wall herself, telling me to go in the house where my books and lessons were, adding that Asmahan died young because she never knew God and that too much distraction will ruin girls and lead to their demise.

In Mombasa I spend my time with Samuel. When he's finished with the gardening, he comes into the house at my request and he prepares some food that I share with him. He doesn't go straight back to his own house after dinner, but rather to night school where he's learning to draw.

In the beginning I found my house in Mombasa strange, for no reason except that to me it was like a prickly pear planted in the sand. Only the green garden that ends in a low fence separates the house from the ocean. It's strange how precisely the sandy coast borders the garden. From the moment I arrived at this house that I'm meant to call my home, I passed my days hunting for comparisons between Mombasa and Beirut. Both have endured successive attacks that make each

city what it is. Both extend along the sea. Beirut's sea
never changes, though. Its water isn't stingy; it doesn't
recede. It isn't surprising and it doesn't frighten. The ebb
and flow of the tide interests me. I've never seen this
before, I tell Chris. But he laughs and says that all the
seas of the world have tides. Beirut's sea is no exception.
Yes, it is! I tell him angrily, as if he is extracting
something from inside me, from my memory, and I don't
want to share it with him. Chris tells me that the waters
of the Mediterranean are exactly the opposite of how I
think of them. He tells me that sailors of all civilizations
from the time of Homer onward were afraid of the
Mediterranean because it was so changeable, always
unpredictable. Sailors on the oceans, by contrast, knew
what was hiding beneath them before they entered deep
waters.

I know what Chris really wants to say—he's talking
about me. But I won't get into another conversation in
which his patience and tolerance will surely get the better
of me. And this won't change my opinion about either the
sea or my life with him. I get up from my chair to walk
around the house and exhale smoke from my cigarette,
which I am constantly relighting. I reach the back garden,
searching for Samuel, and don't find him. I hear a song in
Swahili from behind the garden wall and I approach the
entrance to the garden, knowing that Samuel has arrived.
Chris's voice comes from the garden, strong and resolute—
no doubt he's started to get angry. "You're not in Beirut
anymore, you're here now," he says. He follows up in a voice
meant to leave the impression that this is his final word and

he won't go back on it: "We shouldn't need so many reasons to love a place and call it a homeland."

Mombasa's morning sea is never the same. Since I arrived, the only persistent sight is of the local merchants displaying their wares right on the sands of the beach, when the tide is out and the water has withdrawn back into the heart of the ocean. They come in the morning or at noon when the water's receded, slipping down onto the beach over the edge of the coastline. They can't come down on the roads that lead to the houses gathered on a patch of land planted with trees. These two-story houses are all alike, as though one architect built the same structure a bunch of times. There are many dogs here, dogs trained to attack strangers. Their owners bring these dogs from faraway countries to live with them in big houses they intend to live in forever. The local merchants are frightened of the dogs and the owners of the houses. The foreigners know little about the original inhabitants of this country; their curiosity is limited to expanding their businesses into more and larger markets.

The truth is that people from this country also don't know much about these foreigners, who come here from a number of different countries. The few things that they do know keep them far away from the gates of the big houses. They do know, however, a lot about nature—its changes and fluctuations. They fear nature less than they fear us, the foreigners in their country. They know the ocean's movements, the speed of the wind and the changing weather. They know the times of the high and low tides. They choose six hours when the water is low, far from the coast, and then send their goods down on quickly made ropes that are tied to short poles haphazardly planted in the white sand. There they hang their brightly dyed cloth and small wooden crafts, which are both simple and harsh, like their lives. Some of them stand, holding the colored cloth and soft handmade straw and leather shoes they're selling. They set out displays of suitcases and hats. Rarely do they ask for money in exchange for these things. Instead they prefer gym shoes and T-shirts with advertising slogans for soft drinks printed on them. They trade their handcrafts for things made in China with pictures of Coca-Cola and Pepsi cans, or of people smiling while devouring Kentucky Fried Chicken and McDonald's. Sometimes they ask for alcohol and tobacco.

In Kenya, I spend my time filling my head with things I've received from Lebanon: recently published novels and poetry collections and magazines and short stories and newspapers and studies about the war and the post-war and the Ta'if Agreement and the devastation of 1982 and the Sabra and Shatila trials and the Oslo Accords and the Iran–Iraq War and the siege of Iraq. I don't leave Mombasa much—from time to time I fly to Nairobi just to pick up parcels and packages from Lebanon. In the beginning, I waited in Mombasa for them, for my things to be flown from Nairobi to Mombasa. But things would go missing, especially things like araq and rose water and some of the cassette tapes with Arabic songs and music, or other things Olga sent me.

In Kenya I live every day as if there were no tomorrow, or as if the future right in front of me is still waiting on something from the past. I remember all this now, Olga's question stuck in my mind, the one she repeats on the phone, "What's new? Have you found happiness or are you remembering it, or are you waiting for it… or are you living it?" She asks this knowing full well that happiness is something we only remember and never live: it's pointless to ask someone whether she's happy.

Trees die in Kenya. No, they don't die. People die long before them. The average lifespan here is 40. As soon as I arrived I should have tried to get used to this place, to free myself of the clinging feeling of being a tourist. I carry a transistor radio around with me and go out into the garden in the early hours of morning. At this time of day, I can listen to news from Lebanon on the medium-wave broadcasts. I walk on the damp sand, carrying my radio with me. The news of the war in Lebanon reaches me as if it were a daily destiny. I listen to the news from Beirut as if it could put happiness on pause, like a stop sign. One news report after another with happiness hanging between them… the news of misery that I know too well and from which I have yet to emerge. Misery clings to my skin and my soul, inescapable and viscous. The water recedes far out into the depths of the ocean. The sudden distance of the water frightens me as much as it excites me. An ocean without water is frightening; it's like a desert, stars in the sky lighting up its sands. I see myself, a barefoot woman, hands empty except for a small battery-powered box that brings me news from Lebanon. I walk on the white sand while the water is still out deep in the ocean. My naked feet sink into the moist sand. A warm dampness spreads from my feet to my lower back and I shudder. I'm afraid of myself and my deep desire to enter the labyrinth of the desert and the sea. But I carry on walking. I walk far from the depths of the ocean that appears as white as a face that's deathly ill, or a guest preparing to leave. But all of a sudden the water returns, surprising me. Without warning, I discover that I'm far from the shore and I find myself right in the water, my wet nightgown clinging to my shivering body, my small radio emitting unintelligible signals.

Thus I'm returning to Beirut to sell the building and then return to Mombasa. I have spent more than eleven years traveling between Australia and Kenya, almost as long as I've been married to Chris. Chris was my father's GP. He left his clinic in Australia for Kenya two months after our wedding to direct a British research association that's working to develop a vaccine against malaria, the virus that kills so many people across this vast, poor country. I began my second immigration—from Australia to Kenya—to follow Chris.

I don't refuse Nour's invitation to share a taxi from the Beirut airport. "I left my little notebook on the plane!" I shriek while getting into the taxi. Nour steps back from the taxi door, saying that he'll go back into the airport to ask about it. "Forget about it... Just forget it!" I say hopelessly, waving in his direction, gesturing at him to get into the car. As though what I've written in this notebook is no longer important. As though I've started to accept loss as natural, something I can never change. But then I remember that this notebook of observations contains everything about Joe—the last time we met, our break-up and my return to Beirut. I've written there about my desire for children and my perpetual failure to get pregnant. I've written about the boredom that almost pains me when Chris and I go to bed together. I persevered and wrote everything in Arabic. I find Arabic letters and words exciting in a strange city like Mombasa. Particularly because then I don't worry about Chris finding my notebook some day and reading what I've written.

When I arrive in Beirut, I don't go straight to the building where we used to live before we emigrated to Australia. This is the building that I've come back to reclaim after receiving a letter from Olga saying that the Ministry of the Displaced was offering financial compensation to internally displaced families to vacate houses they occupied during the war. I pass nearby the house in Zuqaq al-Blat but I don't want to get closer. I tell Nour that I miss the intensity of my relationship to my house as it was. And it's changed. Instead of visiting our two-story house that's still occupied by displaced people, I ask the driver to take me to my grandmother Nahil's house in the mountains. On my way up the mountain, the view of rocks and rough terrain—a land rich with images and colors—is repeated over and over. People think that this area has no vegetation. But it produces many-colored rocks and their outgrowths, fertile rocks with little, tough trees growing from them whose leaves stay green all year round.

Nahil doesn't recognize me when she first sees me. She greets me coldly and with a whisper asks Olga about me, while covering her face with a cloth that she lifts over her lips while she asks Olga who I am. "It's Myriam!" says Olga, who has lived with my grandmother Nahil since childhood. She embraces me and directs seemingly pointless words at Nahil, "What's the matter with you? Did you forget your granddaughter Myriam? She's your son Salama's daughter!" Nahil's face lights up when she hears my name. She lifts her head toward me and straightens herself up so that she can reach out and touch my hair. Her thin hand brushes over my hair, down my neck, and she kisses me. "Dark-skinned with big, beautiful eyes!" she says to me in a weak, broken voice. Then she smiles and repeats as she always used to that I'm still beautiful like her, even if I am built like my mother and not slender. I know that some things about me have changed. I've dyed my hair a deep aubergine color, I weigh seven kilos more than I did, I am fifteen years older than the last time she saw me. I've crossed the threshold of forty; I've started putting on make-up before leaving the house. But despite all this, I think that I haven't changed that much and that everyone will still recognize me. I'm sure they'll recognize me by my big, black eyes… that's what I think, but perhaps I'm wrong. Does my face truly betray me? It's true, I haven't endured what others have… does my long absence betray me? Do I seem so strange because I don't share this collective memory? A memory that should show in my movements, the way I walk, and my speech. Did the intensification of violence during my absence distance me this much from the people I love? Did it deprive me of all intimacy and collective memory? Does absence not merely erase the memory of the absent person, but also the memory of the person waiting for her?

She wouldn't leave with us. She says that life here is no different than people's lives elsewhere. Though she's never traveled, she can imagine the cities of the whole world. She can imagine the people there—how they cross the streets and wear their clothes and what they eat. She doesn't need to go anywhere to understand all that, she sees it all from her spot in her mountain house. After the death of my grandfather Hamza, Nahil returned to this mountain house and stayed here, leaving the house in Zuqaq al-Blat to my father. She carries the whole world in her soul without ever changing her location. She never goes to see anything. She says that she can imagine everything. She invents her own pictures from the news and the images on the television that she has finally allowed into her room. I return and find Nahil exactly as I've imagined her, surrounded by religious books handwritten in a large script I can't decipher. She is sitting in her bed, the Hikmeh in her hands. It wasn't easy for her to get a hold of this book—when my grandmother requested a handwritten copy of the Hikmeh, the presence in the house of a Christian, Olga, created some difficulties for the Druze religious men. I've never turned the pages of the Hikmeh in my life. My mother had one but it disappeared when we left the house in Zuqaq al-Blat after my brother Baha''s death. The bombs started falling on the roofs of the buildings and we had to flee our home to take refuge in the house in the mountains. We left, taking nothing with us except a few clothes, our passports and the documents that we needed to travel.

I come back and find Nahil unchanged, as if she hasn't grown older. A mild case of Parkinson's, which comes and goes, restricts her movements. When it comes on, her whole body shakes and she can't be still. Her head jerks awkwardly to the left and right, her tongue gets thick but she insists on talking. She hasn't changed, though she's started covering her head with a long, white mandil. In my memory, she's a woman who never covered her head, her thick, wavy hair that's a color between gray and black. She would go out without her head covered even in the winter, leaving her white mandil draped over her shoulders. She went out like that, in front of people, without a care and then came back all wet, soaking from head to toe. Her face would glow a little then return to normal, though deep in her womb a little climax had burst forth, then just as quickly dried up and disappeared. She wasn't afraid of anyone and in fact felt she was stronger than everyone else. Perhaps these feelings were simply the result of what people used to say about her. She could be stronger than everyone else because they knew about her powerful curses. "God save us from Nahil's curses!" is what people said. They'd say this and repeat the famous tale about the army officer her curses killed.

This was in 1958, when a soldier entered the house by force to arrest my father and interrogate him about a shooting in Hadath. The soldier pushed my father roughly to get him into the jeep. My grandmother Nahil went to talk to the officer who'd remained sitting in the jeep, urging him to release my father, begging him to let him stay with his family because he was an only son, with no brothers, and because his wife, that is to say my mother Nadia, was that very day about to give birth to her second child, my brother Baha'. But the officer wouldn't listen to Nahil and she started assailing him with curses, a group of people gathering around her: "May curses befall you and go with you to your grave... May they go with you to your grave..." She repeated this over and over, holding her head in her hands as if she were afraid it would fall off. My father wasn't detained long, but he did receive many blows to the head there. And my brother was born while my father was in prison. The men of the family always say that on the day my father was released, the soldier entered the officer's room to bring him his usual cup of coffee and found him dead in his bed.

Nahil laughs when she hears these accounts of her power to affect the destinies of men. One day, before my brother Baha' was killed, she told me, "There's no magic, none at all, don't believe it, it's all lies. It's just that there hasn't been any goodness in this house for a long time, even before the war started."

This is what she told me, adding that since she moved to Beirut and stopped visiting al-Sayyid Abdullah and the Prophet Job's holy tomb in the mountains, a series of crises have befallen not only this house but also its family's health, finances and offspring. My grandmother then criticized my mother, saying that my mother had taught us nothing about religion, that she never opened the

Hikmeh even once, though it's constantly been in her sight. Nadia never answered these accusations. It's as though she didn't care, as though neither Nahil nor anyone else could touch on what actually preoccupied her. Nahil never once said that it was because of how Hamza lived his life that the family left religion; she has never made such an accusation. I've always believed, however, that Hamza was extremely far from any kind of belief in the presence of the sacred. From the stories we've heard about him, it seems to me he was always ready to defile anything sacred to fulfill his own ambitions. Hamza lived his life convinced that life on earth was both paradise and hell, that people's lives begin and end here—that the things we don't live don't exist. He used to say that, on the whole, people are a bunch of errors and mistakes. This view of life and the world is his legacy to his son Salama... and then it was our turn, Baha''s and mine. Hamza didn't realize that we no longer believe in the idea of prophets or holy men because of this inheritance, his way of thinking.

My grandmother has lived her whole life making a place for the sacred in our house, but it has vanished, its place taken by an existential anxiety that sleeps in our beds and shares our dreams. Thinking about this always takes me back to my mother Nadia's silence. Sometimes my imagination starts working and I say that Nadia is silent not because of my brother's death but because she can't be a prophet like a man can. Her words will never be carved into the walls of the house so all our visitors can read them. Her silence is simply a protest against this. One evening, in our secret apartment near the Arab university, I found myself asking Georges why I couldn't be a prophet, but a man could. He didn't answer and instead jokingly whispered things like, "Why aren't your questions ever like other women's questions?" "How did my luck bring me a woman like you?" he asked theatrically, lifting his hands up as though imploring a third party there in the room with us... that third person being God! He approached me, bent over and kissed my lips, "You're my very own prophet!" he said and sprang onto the bed. I didn't feel his words or kisses because at that moment my head was filled with the question of prophethood!

Throughout my childhood and adolescence, Nadia's silence preoccupied me; I couldn't understand why she wouldn't stand up to Nahil and defend herself. Why does she never say anything but the words necessary to run our household affairs, words to do with food, health and school? I never know if she's happy or joyful, sad or in pain. She never once talks about what she's feeling. Only about things outside of her body and soul. Things she has no relationship to. To me, Nadia's like a visitor to earth— she doesn't want to change anything, inherit anything or leave anything behind; she doesn't want to take or to give. When I think about her now, the only impression I have is the one she gave us: that she had no power or strength and that we could take advantage of her—in the way that all children my age and my brother's age take advantage— we could do what we wanted and we could tell her anything we wanted. Perhaps my mother's silence is derived from her belief that perfection is found only in religious books; it has no relationship to real life. In this way, she isn't so different than my grandfather and his opinions of the world we live in. She is different from him, though, because she sees and knows and doesn't do anything. I have never once seen Nadia read the Hikmeh. I've seen her read newspapers, novels, magazines and any kind of stories that fall into her hands. Deep inside of herself she believes that religion is love. That's what she gives us, unconditional love, nothing else.

I return to Mombasa from South Africa. My Austrian neighbor Eva accompanies me with new environmental books about droughts and deforestation that she's collected from the tables of the conference she attended. She also bears gifts for her husband. She's returning with her two children, who joined her in her free time in the hotel room, the pool and in a rental car on excursions to waterfalls and shopping. I return with a small half-empty suitcase and a puppy that was a gift from Joe. When I'm with Eva, I long for the feeling of being a mother. I long to feel as I would have if I'd kept my baby and not had an abortion, out of fear of people in Beirut and the scandal. Ever since then I've wanted to recover and I haven't been able to.

The migraine follows me like it's my shadow. I hurry to my bed, which I've truly missed. Chris comes over to me, trying to flirt with me. He wraps his arms around me and draws me to him while trying to pull off my nightgown. My body resists, it wraps around itself like someone closing a window they'd left unlocked. I cover my body completely and tell him that my migraine hasn't relented for even one minute. I tell him this because I know it's the only way to keep him off of me. I have avoided him since I learned from my doctor that I can't conceive. He asks me, flirtatiously, if I met anyone I was attracted to there; in the voice of someone who's given up, he adds that he wouldn't have a problem with it. I don't answer but when hovering between sleep and waking I think that my loneliness when I'm with him has begun to tire him—my loneliness that he prefers to call fidelity, refusing to pursue short-lived affairs when I'm away. The heaviness of our mute relationship exhausts him, since, in his heart of hearts, he believes that life should not be so serious. But he prefers to play his role— the role of husband. In that moment, I think that I'm there beside him by accident, hanging on only because of an arbitrary equation: I don't love him enough to forget that I was left hanging, always waiting to leave, and I don't hate him enough to leave.

This means it is over, the relationship is over!

"This means the relationship's over…" Eva says when I tell her how I feel, as though she's discovered something important.

But who said anything about a lack of love or the end of the relationship? I ask her, thinking that I'm passing through something normal, like the movement of water in the ocean near my house in Mombasa, the ebb and flow of the tide. What I'm living isn't lack of love or the relationship's end. No… no, not at all. It's just a perpetual, repeated, never-ending tidying up of my emotional house.

In the beginning of my marriage to Chris, I thought that
our lack of understanding was born of our two different
languages, and that clarity and honesty would fix this. But
I've discovered that my style only widens the gulf between
us; my clarity ends any ambiguity about whether we might
build something together and ensures that the problem
isn't misunderstanding, but an estrangement that will only
increase with time and take us down a path from which
there is no return.

"Lost in translation!"

He always throws this cliché in my face, naively trying
to lay the blame on our different languages. He'll say it
over and over, trying to find common points between us,
but this expression feels like an insult to me. Whenever
he says it I feel like he's swearing at me. The problem isn't
the difference in language but a lack of language. This
misunderstanding used to exhaust me but in time I
surrendered to it. "Surrender" isn't the right word. Indeed,
I could almost say that misunderstanding has become a
source of amusement for me, so much so that I have begun
to use intentionally few words. It took a long time for me
to discover the pleasure of vagueness. This discovery was
accompanied by another discovery: that I need and miss
the pleasure of a man who makes me laugh. When I
realized this, I started laughing spontaneously, leaving
Chris to guess at the reason for my laughter. I knew this
would irritate him and eventually he'd give up. In the end
he has gotten used to it.

He has begun attributing my behavior to our different
experiences of married life. His first marriage to a British

woman and second to an Iranian woman seem to make him believe that our misunderstandings result from my lack of experience, my failure to understand marriage and relationships between couples. It's hard to know what his marriage to a third woman who is a different age and has different experiences and a different culture than his previous two wives means to him. But I know that he doesn't miss me when I'm traveling. And I miss so many things and live with so much loss that this fact just becomes a part of my life. I know, though, that he'll always write me many letters. Letters that will tell me about his day and then always linger over memories we share... Like how we met for the first time in the airport, when the Australian police called him to search my father—the shrapnel lodged in my father's head made the electronic security checkpoint beep every time my father passed through it. Chris will write to me about the second time we met, in his clinic, and how he used to visit us to follow up on my father's health after we moved out of my uncle's house to our own place in Adelaide.

The first time we met, he entered the room next to the police office in the Australian airport and immediately walked up to my father and me, saying hello and apologizing for being late because of an emergency at the hospital. I no longer remember what he first said to my father when he learned that we'd arrived recently from Lebanon, but he told us that he too was born there and he knew the village of Shemlan, but that he hadn't visited since he left Lebanon in 1958. He remembered people from Shemlan whom my father also knew.

My father was always relaxed and less worried when Chris visited. Chris would go over to my father and pat his shoulder like an affectionate father. A relationship sprang up between them, and quickly it seemed as though they'd been friends for a long time. My father never seemed as sick when Chris was there telling him stories that happened in Lebanon a long time ago, before I was born. Chris would visit frequently to check on his health and play backgammon with him, a game which Salama had practically abandoned after my brother Baha"s death. I imagined that having Chris with us might heal the wounds of our family, stricken with death and loss. This was how a relationship developed between us, between Chris and me. I didn't want it to be anything more than a friendship; with time it transformed into a comforting habit, with no passion or desire. I remember the first meeting of our bodies—he asked me if he could take off his clothes. I found this strange and amusing. We got married four years after I arrived in Adelaide, after I'd lost any hope of seeing Georges ever again. My marriage to Chris is like a compensation for the care and concern that he gives my father, whose madness it's become difficult for me to bear on my own. And I want to have a child to fill the place of the baby I'd lost in Beirut—the fetus I had to abort to avoid the scandal.

My marriage emerged less out of love than conviction. Eva says it's the kind of marriage that "clears up unresolved life issues," like companies managing the clearance of imported cargo shipments. Eva also considers my marriage to be linked to the past more than the future.

I tell her that perhaps she's right. What I feel for Chris isn't love, being with him instead gives me more of a fabricated feeling of serenity. I've discovered that this serenity does not come from Chris himself—his personality or characteristics—but from the terrible circumstances all around me. These circumstances have changed the course of my life and transformed me from a woman who dreamed about the future to a woman who simply tries to repair a present that's distorted by the past.

The two of us, Chris and I, exist in different worlds. When I tell Eva this, I add that I'd reckoned that after our marriage I'd sleep better and my fears would leave me. But instead I'm still anxious—when I'm near him, when he isn't around, when he's away. Our lack of understanding, my loneliness, how far I am from my friends in Beirut— all of this makes me anxious. Eva is making bread with candied fruit in it and stops, turning off the noisy electric mixer so she can tell me that I'm too philosophical. With the back of her damp, dough-covered hand, she pushes strands of blonde hair from her forehead. She adds that I'm surely mad. This is her response to what I've said about how I can't understand why Chris loves me and how strange it is that I can never understand his way of loving me. I tell her whenever I think about Chris I feel as if I'm an exotic fruit; he desires it when he finds it within his reach, but can forget it just as quickly when it isn't there. I always have to be this exotic fruit, despite myself. I have to be that Oriental woman, coming from the other side of the sea, who is nothing like the women in his family. I discovered this game quickly, though, and I withdrew. I withdrew and said nothing to him. Perhaps what surprises him is that I'm not at all like the women of *1,001 Nights*. I don't tell him tales so that he can sleep and I can save myself. I rely on silence to rescue me. Perhaps this is what spoils the tacit agreement we've had in place since we married. I think that when I travel to Beirut he'll write me many letters, but I won't write back. If I have to choose between exchanging letters and talking to Chris on the phone—if conversation is unavoidable—I'll choose the phone, if only because that can be finished quickly and no traces of it remain. It's as if my life with him is nothing but a hole in the sand. Eva collects all the kitchenware that she's used to make the cake, puts it into the dishwasher, and says, "You're mad! Everything you're saying is just rhetoric... completely disconnected from real life."

Throughout all our years together in Kenya, Chris persists in repeating that he loves me and could never live with another woman. Despite this, he keeps protesting against everything I do or say, using my changeable moods as justification. Perhaps he's right. I often feel that I can't decide my position on things; I'm not sure how to see the world. How do you describe twilight, for example? Is it when darkness begins or is it what remains of the light of day? Or is it both at once? At times I've understood the differences between us as between two contrasting personalities—the first builds a sense of stability by believing that what he was told and taught is absolutely, indisputably true. He believes that what he's learned is enough. The second person, on the other hand, has lost all hope of stability, to the point that existence itself is a source of doubt and questioning. I'm this second person. My inability to plan summer vacations enrages him. He'll ask me to decide how and when we'll travel to Australia to see his children in Sydney and to see my parents in Adelaide. Or he'll ask me to plan a trip to another country. And I'll always answer, "We'll figure it out tomorrow." He thinks my answers mean I don't care, but I'm never entirely certain if tomorrow will come. I tell him that life in Lebanon never allowed me to plan more than a month in advance, how does he expect me to decide how we'll spend the summer holidays when it's still February? I tell him that planning is a whole culture that I'm not used to and he has to understand this. I tell him that my brother Baha' was getting ready for a relaxing trip to Istanbul, his ticket in his pocket, when he was killed. In my excuses he'll find another reason to prolong the conversation. My pleas just provoke him and he doesn't understand them—like all people who've never lived through war. He'll tell me that I'm far away from Lebanon now… now it's time to forget, to get used to my life with him in Australia or Africa. Sometimes he'll explain away my bad moods by saying that they come from the dark clothes I wore after Baha''s death. But this too is a way of life that's hard to change—I no longer know how to buy brightly colored clothes. Why do you wear this dark dress? You look miserable in it. Why don't you eat cold meat and sausage with me for breakfast? Is there something troubling you? Did Olga say something on the phone that upset you? Did you visit your doctor today? Which one—

the psychologist or the gynecologist? How's your Arabic teaching? Your English teaching? He'll repeat these questions over and over. When my answers are improvised and short and don't add or change anything, he leaves.

I've often decided that I should make more of an effort to improve my situation and my relationship to the world, as well as my relationship to Chris and our social life. After weeks of this effort, though, he'll suddenly tell me that there's no point in exhausting myself, he knows that I have no desire whatsoever to go out to dinner with him, his friends and their women, especially because I always have to speak a language that's not my own. He seems to understand, but I feel that this understanding hides a bitter disappointment he's trying to summon the patience to tame. When the results of his research in the laboratory are unsatisfactory, he tries to suggest that his work has deteriorated because he worries about me too much and can't sleep. I'm always the reason for any setback that he or his work suffers. When we were newly married, I would believe everything he said. I felt hugely guilty and gave all of my time to him. This meant that I was at home most afternoons, spending my time reading and writing—writing things no one but Olga ever read. While Chris was out working and earning money, I would spend my morning hours teaching English in courses designed to wipe out illiteracy in Mombasa, as well as giving private Arabic lessons. After years of this, I've become convinced that he invests all his energy into his work. The very moment he leaves home, he forgets the place he's just been, forgets who's in it, forgets me. I'm convinced that the unsatisfactory results of his work are because of him alone and have no connection whatsoever to me. Yet whenever the issue of his work is raised with his friends or colleagues, he mentions my perpetual sadness.

Chris counts the number of people infected with malaria and tries to save them, while I'm infected by the malady of mute rage, compounded by fear. He won't be able to save me. My illness requires playfulness and Chris isn't good at playing. He doesn't know how to play. He doesn't even play with the puppy, which he began to fight with the moment I brought it back from South Africa. As if he knew who I got it from and desperately wants to get rid of it. Play is humankind's most important invention, Samuel says, rubbing his face on the dog Yufu's head, and it's not only human, he continues, watch! See how animals love to play! Samuel tells me, raising his voice as though he's learned that I only listen to him when he changes the tone of his voice, shaking me out of my deep thoughts and forcing me to pay attention. Chris doesn't play... He has his habits. Here's a day of his habits: going to the laboratory at seven thirty, coming back at one, sleeping after lunch, going back to the laboratory from three thirty until seven.

No doubt malaria is on the rise because of these habits, because it has gotten used to his habits!

As for me, I'm not sure of anything. I can accept and refuse something with equal ease. The more years I live in Mombasa, the more difficult I find it to have habits. But what does is it mean to be a woman without habits, not even drinking coffee in bed? He comes to me, sure that the hand he rests on my shoulder has the magic of the serums that he spends his whole day with in the lab. He loses his patience after a few minutes and leaves after I say for the thousandth time that I miss playing, that play is ageless and that I'm slowly dying here. He leaves me and goes out. I walk over and turn on the tape recorder so that Asmahan's voice will rise out of it, reverberating in revenge. I go back to the book that I had in my hand before Chris entered. I read, "Nietzsche was right when he said that original sin pushed us toward a perpetual feeling of hatred, and that 'god' is a lethal invention—it's difficult to believe in a god who doesn't dance."

I narrated my Beirut and Australia lives to Eva, my neighbor in Mombasa. Now that I've returned to Beirut, it's easy to narrate my Kenya tales to Olga, whom I missed and who missed me. But why do I remember all this now, when it's behind me? Is it because the past remains forever part of our future and never goes away? I narrate my life in Kenya to Olga, thinking of Nour and what's happened between us. Meeting him has been something strange. As though I left Kenya and came back specifically to find him—not to reclaim the house that I'd lost. I've returned to Beirut in search of a dancing god, but found instead a companion for my journey of loss.

Chris sends me a second letter. I've only been here two months. I feel like he wrote all his letters before even I left him.

I don't like visiting Australia with Chris because I have to spend so much time traveling with him from one city to another to visit his children and family. He insists that I accompany him when I just want to stay at home with my mother and listen to what she tells me about my father, herself and her work. We speak English together, my mother and I, and it doesn't bother me. It's enough that she's speaking again, it doesn't matter in what language. The last time I visited Adelaide, Nadia greeted me with less silence, with words that I'd missed from her for so long. We hugged as if each of us had found the other after having been lost. She's taken intensive English classes and her silence disappears completely when she speaks a foreign language. A few years ago she started working part-time in an organization that looks after immigrants who come from countries that have gone through civil wars. She gave me a small gray cat, saying that she found it that morning. She brought it in, washed it, fed it, and gave it an English name, Gray, because of its color. A cat to replace her cat, Pussycat, in Beirut. I was happy for my mother, who looked like a girl suddenly taking her first steps. My mother has gotten used to her life in Australia and when I read something to her about Lebanon, she tells me that she doesn't want to hear anything and never wants to go back.

I take Nadia and Salama to the public park. Salama arrives a few steps ahead of us and enters the park, greeting the gatekeeper and the cleaners. He doesn't sit with us for long, but gets up and starts walking back and forth from left to right across the park. "They respect me more here.

I feel like I am a respected human being here," he always says to me, while engaged in what seems to be his only hobby in Adelaide—constantly, never-endingly, crossing the street. He goes out and steps into the crosswalk; drivers are surprised by him and slam on their brakes so they won't run him over. Cars stop for him and my father completes his journey to the other sidewalk, joyful and proud. The cars then take off, their drivers cursing and swearing at him in English, which doesn't bother my father. He doesn't understand what's happening around him. All he knows is that the whole world stops for him the moment he leaves home or the park for the street. Cars stop for him and then continue, then other cars come and stop and then continue. Salama keeps on crossing the street going from one sidewalk to the other. The signal changes from red to orange then to green and Salama continues his game, the cars honking. A man sticks his head out a car window and starts cursing Salama, who doesn't understand what's being said to him. In fact, he looks forward and just keeps walking. He stops when he gets angry, in the middle of the street, to tell the driver who hurls his words into the air, "You don't know who you're talking to, boy!" It doesn't take long for these short bursts of anger to change into smiles. Salama smiles at the brightly colored cars that shine even when the sun disappears. Cars shine in the shade like the eyes of Beirut's street cats. But he isn't in Beirut, I think while sitting near my mother, who's reading her book.

My mother has gotten used to my father's madness and accepts it as her lot in life. I keep a careful eye on him, his mouth agape with a wide smile. All the while Salama keeps moving ceaselessly between the two sidewalks. I can't keep watching him; I turn away from him as though his movements are an affliction. "Leave him, leave him be," my mother, who's used to his madness, tells me, "don't worry." It's raining hard but my father doesn't care. It's July, the height of summer, he says, the rain's just fleeting and it'll pass quickly. My father never accepts that it's winter in July and that rain lasts for months here. He lifts his head toward the gray sky, where there are clouds that can't reach him and words that still trouble him, the words of my grandfather Hamza, which remain planted in his mind, body and soul. Hamza is dead but Salama has never healed from the violence of these words. Even though these violent words can no longer reach him, he hasn't healed. I leave the wooden bench on the sidewalk and walk toward him, while my mother takes shelter in a small kiosk in the center of the park, fleeing from the rain. I try to grab my father. But he keeps walking back into the crosswalk, heading from one side of the street to the other, rain completely soaking his clothes. I don't know what to do. I look for my mother and see her running toward us, holding her book over her head to keep it from getting wet. I hold onto my father's arm, water pouring down from his hair into his eyes and over his face. My mother reaches us and extends her arm to Salama and meekly he stops moving, muttering unintelligible words. He holds onto Nadia's arm and the three of us pass through the neighborhood park in Paradise, crossing the street while my mother takes the house key out of her purse, saying that it'll be night soon and we should get back.

In the first days after my return to Lebanon I have to prepare a number of legal documents to present to the Ministry of the Displaced. They tell me that it's a matter of days. But now I've been in Beirut for more than three months and am still filling out forms whose purpose I can't understand. The last forms I had to fill out were exactly the same as the ones I'd filled out the time before. When I let the government employee see my irritation and bewilderment, he answers me with open sarcasm, "Don't worry, ma'am, you can practice your writing skills."

Why did I come back? I ask, blaming myself and cursing the employee. Why am I here? I could've assigned my power of attorney to Olga or someone else. But they'd asked for my father to come in person because someone wants to buy the building and tear it down to build a big new one in its place. This building will overlook Beirut's downtown, destroyed by the war, which a private company is now undertaking to rebuild. My father is lost in his insanity, however, and it took days to prepare him for our visit to the notary in Adelaide where he could sign over his power of attorney to me so I could take care of this.

When I first arrived in Beirut, I didn't see anyone. There were only Nour's visits, which have increased until they're pretty much every day. The apartment I've rented is small, lost at the end of a corridor on the second floor of a neglected building near the American university. When there's a knock on the door, I can't imagine who would visit me today. It's Nour. He hugs me as though he's known me for a long time. I'm happy that I've met him, it's as if he'd been waiting for me here. This man comes as a surprise to me. His visits are what I needed to connect to Beirut—meeting a man who has also come back to search for a lost connection. We leave my apartment and walk toward the sea; the autumn chill is mild. Nour draws close to me and puts his arm around my shoulder for a quick moment, then pulls away. It's as though he wants to say something but has changed his mind, or perhaps suddenly feels that he's hurrying something by showing his emotions. I feel at once anxious and slightly hopeful. I want him to leave his hand on my shoulder and tell me, without thinking, what he's feeling.

Autumn in Beirut is strange. The day begins with promising sunshine, a sky that makes your eyes tear up because it's so clear and blue. Clouds spread out around the edges of the sky like a picture frame; it's strange how Beirut's autumn changes its colors so quickly. The sky's frame widens and slowly sweeps away what was inside it. Then clouds cover the sky; without notice they change from white to translucent gray, accumulating and growing darker. The wind picks up suddenly as though it had been concealed beneath the roots of the city's few remaining trees. It starts from the earth and rushes upward. Docile Sunday Beirut. Someone who's seen this wouldn't believe that sleeping Beirut could wake up each morning and produce such violence from within its walls. Every day, it spreads out its violence in the broad daylight, like women laying out an entire season's clothes under the sun's rays.

Sunday is Beirut's day off. It's as if violence has a day off too, as if its buildings are taking a break from the voices that breach their yellowing walls. Sunday mornings are silent except for the distant sounds of soulless church bells, turned on with the push of a button. These sounds are met, not too far away, by the prayers of muezzins. The city is sleeping today and so is the sea. I'm reconciling with Beirut today. Beirut has changed. It's another city. I only feel intimate with it on Sundays. That's when my city returns to being itself.

On Monday, Nour comes to take me out to dinner. He makes me laugh when he tells me that he's missed me since yesterday, that I've become his only connection to Beirut. I imagine that Beirut would be lonely for someone like him who doesn't have old friends or family here. Our dinner changes from an ordinary event into an interview. He tells me that he's writing about Lebanese who've returned after the war and wants to interview me. I can't find anything to tell him. It's as if I've lost the ability to speak, especially after he comments on my silence and I see him taking out his notebook to transcribe some of the words I've used to describe my return to Beirut.

Nour and I have to see each other every day so that he can finish what he was telling me. Most of the time we meet in his little rented office, near where he lives in Ras al-Nabaa. He rents it from a dentist who gave up his practice and went to the Gulf. Last time he asked me to help him interview people who don't know English. It doesn't frustrate me to spend these long periods of time with him. We've even started working late at night. As soon as I enter the office, he pulls a leather chair over next to his, and makes tea. He's started telling me about his private life, intimate things—I've never heard such intimate things about a man before. I've never heard such things because other men haven't meant anything to me; words can't be separated from their owners.

He sits next to me, only a small space between us. I think about Ines, the young woman who sometimes comes to his office to transcribe his voice recordings. She says that she's bored, that the atmosphere in her workplace, a press office, doesn't suit her temperament. She complains, gets up and opens the window to the left of his desk. Then she shuts it, concocting an excuse to come into his room while he brings her a chair like the one he brought me. I see her coming in as I'm going out. Like a teenage girl I wonder... how will he greet her? Will he greet her like he greets me? Will he be confused about where to look, his eyes the color of sea and sky, or let himself gaze at my face? I turn away as though I have all these questions for only a moment. A hidden power will lift me from my chair, pushing me towards him. It propels me to narrow the vast divide between us, the divide that's not even one meter wide.

I call him at the time of our usual morning rendezvous to say we should meet somewhere near the sea instead of working in the office, because the winter sun is brilliant and beautiful today. At the café on the seaside, he takes a sip of caffe latte then suddenly spits it out. He says that he can't drink it, it's made from powdered milk and he wants fresh milk. The waiter doesn't understand what Nour means. "But really, madame, it is fresh, I just mixed it with the water right now!" the waiter says over and over again, directing his words at me and shaking his head like someone unjustly accused, with no hope that I can rescue him.

We then go back to the office and stay there until evening, translating and printing the interviews. He offers to take me home; first we have to walk in the direction of his apartment so that he can get his car. It's raining a little and we go down the long, dark staircase together under his umbrella. I'm struck by a desire to touch him, to smell his scent, but I savor this feeling from a distance. We pass by his ground-floor flat and he wants to show me his garden. A dim light shines through one of the windows facing the garden. I wonder if this light is coming from his bedroom and what his bed is like. I want to go in and look around but I just wait in front of his flat while he brings the car around.

He starts the car and I get in beside him. It begins to rain heavily. I can't hear what he's saying because I'm observing the way his hands move on the steering wheel and am thinking about how little space there is between our bodies. He takes the Corniche road around to Ayn Mreisseh before dropping me off at my place on Makhoul Street. The rain hits the windshield even harder and waves from the sea beat against the asphalt of the Corniche. A moment passes before he turns off the car, opens the door and gets out. He walks around the car and opens the door on my side. I thought that I said I wanted to stay here in the car and meditate on the waves, but I didn't say anything and he couldn't hear what I didn't say. So I get out and look at him. He waves at me and gets back into the car. I walk around to the entrance of my building, my eyes damp with the power of an anxious desire.

Today I should present new documents to the Ministry of the Displaced. I have no desire to go so I call Nour and go out to meet him at his office. I walk a long way on foot before finding a taxi, so I arrive late. It isn't easy to find a servees taxi to take me from Bliss Street to Ras al-Nabaa. I have to get out at Bishara al-Khoury Street and walk. He's buried in work at his computer. I ask him if we can go out because I've started to feel suffocated. He leaves everything and goes with me, leaving his computer on. Before locking the door, he asks me if it's cold outside. I tell him that he's wearing more than enough clothes. He replies, I wonder if I should bring a scarf. I tell him that I once heard him say that he doesn't like the cold, and so he should bring it. He smiles and brings it with him. I like his simplicity. I like his spontaneity. We walk to his car. He once again talks about his work, his interviews, his family, his feeling of exile and uprootedness, his house that he carries on his back like a turtle. The weather is cold and the wind pushes us forward. I enjoy the cold. He gets out of the car near the lighthouse and I suggest that we walk a little here then go and drink tea or coffee at Rawda café. I've always liked that café. Before I left Beirut, I spent a whole winter there in the glassed-in room writing something about the life of others, which is my life. I write and only Olga reads my writing.

Just as we leave the office, a powerful feeling develops between us. And then, just as quickly, it disappears. The visit is urged on by ambiguous desire, a misunderstanding or perhaps wondering on his part: What do I want? Why did I call him to go out, why am I here? I let him wonder about my silence that I don't want to waste. Perhaps my silence encourages him to move his secret contemplation into the realm of questioning. He doesn't ask and I don't want to explain. This time, I'll let my life find its way, I'll throw my desire to the wind that plays on the surface of the water and transforms it into high waves that crash against the café's white walls. I observe him while we sit; I chose the seat where I could see the sea. I don't want to turn my back on it.

A desire more powerful than myself floods me. I give myself to it... it takes me. I no longer see what others see. I let myself give into a desire that I thought I'd lost. How can I know what's inside him? He begins to speak freely. I listen to him with calm contentment. I listen, thinking about him. Just seeing his fingers holding his cigarette, about to light it, makes me shiver. He pauses, then continues what he had started to say. I watch him look at me this same way and forget that I'm holding a cigarette and an unlit match in my fingers. Then I put this all aside and drink my cold tea. It's eight o'clock in the evening when we leave Rawda. I go back to his place with him. Outside the door, I want to tell him, let me into your heart as well as your home. Instead I say, I want to see your little garden this time. But I'm thinking, do I really want to be let into his heart? Will I be able to bear the burden of a relationship? Or do I only want to use my head to survey things a little—to see his place and his life, to see them through my own desires, my body and eyes. I look at him for a long time but then feel annoyed and turn my face to feel the wind coming from the blue line of the horizon.

In his little flat, he goes into the kitchen to prepare dinner for us. I stand and watch him. It's nice, how he busies himself cooking for me. He takes out a bag of frozen seafood and quickly prepares rice and a salad as well. The smells of cooking pervade the kitchen and the whole house. Suddenly I feel hungry. Nour works quickly while my stomach grumbles; I want to eat. I look for a bottle of white wine that he says is at the back of the refrigerator. With the first glass, I feel strongly that I'm living another life. A life that in no way resembles my previous lives in Beirut, Australia or Kenya. My other lives. Lives like my first meeting with Georges, my observations in the notebook that I left on the plane, as if I'd forgotten it on purpose. Lives that begin in two places or more or are from no place. Stories that don't meet up. Lives whose origins are an abundance of love and an abundance of desire, perhaps more than a man can satisfy. Lives for which I open two permanent parentheses in my heart. I open up for him too and invite him inside.

When we embrace, a little question flashes through my mind: Why does his face grow red when our bodies touch? Why do men fear these moments, inviting the whole world's worries into the room to come between us? All my questions disappear in a fleeting moment that accounts for an entire lifetime. A complete passion, which

I once believed that I'd lost forever, takes its place. In the moment, I tell him "I feel like I'm traveling!" I close my eyes. "What's happening between us is better than traveling," he whispers, burying his face in my hair, then kissing my face and neck. Is what is happening to me now like when I first knew Georges? We don't laugh like Georges and I did. Love then was a frivolous game we enjoyed. It was easy, light and painless. Now love means regaining a desire I believed had died long ago. This act isn't free of nostalgia. But I don't know why.

He starts coming to my flat on Makhoul Street every night. The calm apartment transforms into a site of life and celebration. I've never known sex in my life like I experience it with Nour. He cooks for me while I sit in the small living room across from the kitchen and watch him search for the ingredients he needs. He's calm and peaceful standing there. My heart beats with love for him. I love that man when he's cooking for me. My desire for him is mixed with scent memories of the delicious spices that emanated from Nadia's kitchen when I was small. Remembering my mother while a man cooks for me is a wonderful, pleasurable thing. This erases the masculine and feminine roles. Nothing remains between us and with us, except love and desire that is reignited every time it starts to wane. A thread suspended between the sighs of separation and sighs of coming together. A separation delineated only by the distance between two bodies and the time between two moments.

I return to search for a place that I thought I'd lost. Is Nour also searching for a place for himself here? He tells me: I don't belong to any place, not here and not there in that other country where I was raised. I wonder, where we do belong, then? Does belonging have prior conditions? Does moving from place to place, these lives of immigration, diffuse these conditions? Or does immigration not matter? Does belonging to a place give us stability, is instability the reason for our ever-present anxiety? Or is war the reason? Is...? Does...? That anxiety—not just now and not just since I left Beirut, or in Australia, or in Mombasa—follows me like a shadow. Before I left Lebanon I moved from here to there and from there to here. From the mountains to the city I left and then traced my steps back. I found Nahil reading the Hikmeh, or in front of the house throwing food to the birds. I found empty cages whose doors were always wide open. Whenever Abdo, who tended to my grandfather's fields, found a colorful bird he put it in a cage to give it to Nahil, who would immediately take the bird out of the cage, put it on her open hand, hold it in front of her and let it fly away into the sky.

I light a cigarette while still in bed. Nour tells me that he has allergies and can't tolerate smoking in the bedroom, but he will just this one time. I don't answer. I put out the cigarette and ask him if he would drive me the next day to visit Georges' family. He makes some excuses but I repeat my request insistently. He finally agrees!

Olga accompanies us on the visit to Georges' mother. The war prevented us from building a life together in Australia,

Georges and I. Georges' mother is there waiting for me, his sister with her. She's holds a cigarette as if it were the same one she was holding when I bade her farewell fifteen years ago. When she sees me, she cries. She tells me that she's still waiting for him, that she feels close to death and has bequeathed the task of continuing to search for Georges to her daughter. "After the mother, only the sister can pursue this cause." She chokes up as she says this. I cry, too. This moment helps me understand why I came to see her. She's the only person who can allow me, just by seeing her, to finish my ongoing mourning.

On the way back, Olga can't stop talking. It's like she wants to erase all trace of this visit. "The war is over... It's over!" Olga sings, theatrically stretching her arms out of the window of Nour's car, waving her hands outside. "Look at the streets, look at the traffic... All the hotel rooms are booked up!" I don't know at that moment where Olga really is. Is she joking? Or is she making fun of the television channels that rejoice all day long that the war's ended, even though still today men are missing and no one dares ask questions about them. I know that Olga is lying to herself and to us—that she doesn't believe what she's saying at all.

"We're not going to be afraid anymore, the war's over," she continues, pointing out that they took away all the sandbags used at checkpoints—there's only one pile of sandbags left on the Jounieh Highway, near the Nahr al-Kalb Tunnel, and they say that they'll "cleanse" the area soon. Yesterday, they "cleansed" the "Lebanese Forces" areas and arrested a number of them, I say to myself silently.

Before this, a Phalange Party figure disappeared, and they said that the Syrian secret service apparatus had disappeared him. After that another man and another and all of this is happening in a time of peace. "The war is over," I repeat what Olga said soundlessly. I look at her reproachfully, because she doesn't want to see the truth, above all she wants to believe the lies she's repeating. I motion to her to be quiet. Olga quiets down but her words bring me back to a past I want to forget. So why do I blame Olga? I too want to remember the past without pain.

Beirut is heavy with pain. But perhaps Olga is right, what use is memory? A wave from inside the sea should rise up and cleanse everything, wash away tales from the past… its stories, hatreds and resentment. For a moment I live the war as it was then, all that I lived through more than fifteen years before. As though it has been asleep in my body and needs only a little push to reawaken and float up to the surface of my memory. But I want to start over, to open my eyes one morning and see a sun that doesn't remind me of any yesterday or any war.

I return empty-handed to Beirut, where my loss began. That loss is all I have now.

At a certain moment, near the museum, suddenly I ask Nour to stop the car. Many workers, rebuilding, renovations. I recall that this is where I was stopped at the checkpoint. Here! Yes, here! This is where I was stopped at a checkpoint before I left Lebanon. "Get out, you!" he yelled, pointing his machine gun at me. He was the one who stormed the supermarket and took the cartons of children's milk right off the shelves and even out of pregnant women's shopping carts. "Isn't that him, Olga?" I ask her, pointing out the car window. "Look at him, wearing a shirt and tie and putting something on his belt, what is it? A gun?" "No, it's not a gun, it's a mobile phone," Olga replies. "Isn't he the same one who stopped a woman crossing the checkpoint between the museum and Barbir and took three bottles of water she was carrying with her to the West side during the Israeli siege and bombardment of West Beirut, when its water was cut off?

"You sent me stories in the papers, news and pictures... everything. What's happening? Have you forgotten?" I ask her, trying to blink back the tears in my eyes, "Yes, I've forgotten..." Olga replies, seeming bewildered.

"I didn't forget, I didn't forget," I repeat, while Nour just seems afraid of something he can't express. He looks at me and strokes my thigh with the palm of his hand as though he understands what I'm saying.

Olga jumps up from the backseat and holds onto my shoulders impatiently to quiet me down as though I were crazy and raving, "Enough, shut up! You weren't here, I was. I lived the war and I have the right to forget. Three-quarters of the people who keep talking about memory weren't here and didn't see anything... Enough already! We want to forget. Let the people who want to forget, forget. It isn't a crime to forget!" She says this while holding my shoulders tight as if she were afraid for me because of my words. Perhaps she's afraid for herself. She lifts one of her hands from my shoulder and touches my face as though asking me to turn toward her because what she's saying is very important and I need to hear it.

She calms down a little, aware that what she said was hard for me to hear, "There's no point to all this talk. Come on, let's sing Asmahan, you still like her, I know you do!" I tell her that I haven't listened to Asmahan since arriving in Beirut, I left her back in my house in Mombasa. Right then, it's hard for me to remember any of her songs, as if I've completely erased her from my mind. Olga brings her face right up near my hair, puts an arm around my shoulders and whispers, "Of course you aren't hearing her voice!" She regains her loud voice and rebukes me, "Is there anything else in your head to think about besides the war?" I look at her and think that it's her right to scold me. I'm the one who enjoys good health, and she knows deep down that her health won't allow her to live through another war or the peace to come after that war. But she fights desperately to defend a meek, sham peace.

Saying that the war is over is like saying that her health is stable—they are two lies that help her to survive.

Although the war has ended, we still hold on to so much hatred in order to live together. To live in peace. So much hatred for families to continue, for children to grow, for cities to rise and for countries to be built. We need so much hatred just to go on, and when we die no one will know us.

They say the war is over!

I'll never find a place in the world where thoughts and words are as deceptive as they are in Beirut. But despite all this, I find myself implicated here.

I remember what a journalist friend of Nour's said to me when I met him a few days ago, "In Beirut, everything

begins as a drama and transforms into a caricature." Easy
for a journalist to say, I think, and ask him, "Is everything
happening now a caricature, then?"

I start repeating what Olga is saying aloud, as though
they're my own words. The war's over, we won't be afraid
anymore, they took away all the checkpoints, there's only
one sandbag left on the Nahr al-Kalb Highway. They say
that they'll "cleanse" the area soon. I think about what
Olga says and what the journalist says. I tell myself that
in any case, I won't use this road much while I'm in Beirut.
Perhaps I'll take it on one more visit to Georges' family
before I head back to Kenya. But will I return to Kenya,
to my house back in Mombasa?

If only Georges had listened to me the day I left. If
only he'd paid attention. If he'd agreed to travel with
me... perhaps he'd still be here now, perhaps he'd have
saved himself from being disappeared or murdered or
tortured. Perhaps he'd have saved me from a long journey
of waiting and a marriage I didn't want from the very
beginning. From years of doubt and waiting between
Australia and Kenya. I wonder why I insisted that Nour
accompany me on my trip today. Why did I ask him to
come with me to visit Georges' family? Is it because I want
to bury the past with this visit or because I want Nour to
share the past with me?

I met Georges at university but our friendship was
only born when we were working alongside Palestinians
in the Fatah Party. He used to drive every day from his
house in Sinn al-Fil to my house in Zuqaq al-Blat, and
give me a ride to Shatila where we worked as hospital

volunteers. This was when the crossings between the two Beiruts were still open. Later we met as lovers. We met then at Intisar and Malek's house and after that in an apartment that Georges rented for us in the Arab University area near the hospital.

I remember the day when we decided to move to a safer place. We were in Intisar's room and neither of them—that is to say, Intisar and Malek—were home. I was naked and Georges was kneeling, kissing every part of my body, his hand gently stroking my breasts. Suddenly we heard the door open. It was Intisar's sister, who lived with her, coming home from school. We used to remember that first time we met her and laugh about it together.

We ate dinner at the house of a Danish woman who also worked as a hospital volunteer in the Shatila camp. After dinner there once I took off my shoes and left them in the middle of the room near the leg of the dining table. At the end of the night, Georges had to drive me home because the wine had made my head heavy. I asked him to help me get to the car and don't remember what happened on the way. No doubt I fell asleep, since I do remember how he gently stroked my face and shoulders to wake me up, saying, "Myriam, Myriam, come on, we're there." When I didn't answer, he asked jokingly, "Will you sleep at my place?" When I still didn't answer, he said, openly and naughtily, "Will you sleep with me?"

I woke up with all my faculties at that moment as though a bell had suddenly rung inside my head. When I got out of the car he slipped a piece of paper with his phone number on it into my hand, saying, "We've known each other for a while and we don't call each other. I won't call you first, even though I really want to see you again. I'll leave it to you to take the initiative." I was sleepy but awake enough to hear him and like what he said. I liked how simply he said what he wanted.

The next time we met, he told me how my shoes had excited his imagination and a thousand poems that night! He said this laughingly, then stopped and added as though he were reading from a book, "Just seeing one of your shoes upside down turned my whole life upside down, from top to toe!" Rarely did we meet without recalling the memory of that evening. While kissing my body, he'd repeat, "I only had to see one of your shoes, left carelessly on the bare tiles near the table, to imagine you in bed, naked. This was enough to make me desire you, to be aroused and imagine your naked legs clenched around my waist while I'm on top of you."

I started to believe that Georges couldn't have sex without recalling that story. He brought fruit into bed before making love, fed me grapes, kissed me and put his tongue in my mouth to share the fruit. Sometimes, when in bed, I felt we were playing, like children, and that our bodies were finding their way to a pleasure without sin.

Before I left for Australia, we made love early in the morning. This was the most pleasurable time for him.

Relaxed and contented, I whispered to him after we'd finished making love: "I forgive you all your past sins and those which you have not yet committed, from now until five hundred years into the future."

He answered with a laugh, "Yes, yes, my Goddess, my Lord-ess." I used my damp hand to wipe the juices of our lovemaking from between my legs, and told him, "This is the holy water, take it as a baptism." I rubbed my hand on his face and forehead. I told him that rituals, no matter what religion you were raised in, are pure sex. For me, the best moments to make love are during prayer times, since there's so much Sufi ritual in lovemaking.

Georges found my comparison between making love and Sufism strange, and answered with a devilishness that I love, "There are too many holy prayers and rituals... one man alone cannot carry out all your wishes." I said sarcastically, "Yes, there are more than you think, especially if you gather up all the sects in the world and add up all of their required prayers and rituals. For us here in Lebanon, my dear, this won't be easy—it's almost too many to calculate!"

"Luckily, your rituals can be completed without speaking aloud!" he replied, still laughing.

"You're evil and shameless!" I answered, throwing myself on top of him.

The war kidnapped Georges. His family is still waiting for him to come back. He's neither alive nor dead. He's between two places, suspended between war and peace, the past and the present. I remember the day we met in our apartment near the Arab University and I told him that the test I'd taken confirmed I was pregnant and that the doctor had advised me to have an abortion because I was still unmarried and was, as he put it, "a good girl, from a good family, not a slut."

I wanted to shout in the doctor's face but instead I closed my eyes and waited for him to finish what he was saying. Then I removed his hand from my naked belly, got down off the examination table, put on my underwear, and hurried out. After I aborted the baby, I didn't see Georges much for a while. I was angry at him, at myself, at everything. But our separation didn't last long.

After the fall of Tell al-Zaatar, Georges didn't go back very often to the East Beirut neighborhood where he used to live. They knew his face there. He started to be afraid, though his fear didn't prevent his kidnappers from disappearing him. No one knows how he disappeared and when. People say many things... that he was kidnapped in West Beirut, more specifically near our apartment by the Arab University, that he was kidnapped off a boat headed from Beirut to Larnaca, or perhaps just minutes before he was to board the boat.

I have to leave Nour before five in the afternoon. Intisar is waiting for me at the Rawda café. I gently extract my body from his arms. At that moment, I feel like someone returning a stolen love to its rightful owners.

I leave to go meet Intisar and decide to walk between Ras al-Nabaa and Raouche, trying to find my way with considerable difficulty between the forest of cars parked on the sidewalk.

When I arrive at the Rawda café, Intisar is waiting for me there with Malek. I haven't seen them in fifteen years. How much Intisar's changed—her face seems rounder but paler and faded. Her body is thicker and slower moving, but the sparkle in her eyes and her nervous laughter remain a registered trademark of their owner. She hugs me with a shout, "Meemoo, my love!" She always called me that when we were at university. "My God, how much I've missed you!" she carries on, her voice as loud as an explosion. I feel the people around us becoming a big circle that encloses us. Intisar wanted to surprise me and has invited all of our old friends. Laughter and questions and kisses and tears. A hug then an abbreviated life story, still suspended powerfully in memory. Immediately after I left Beirut, I had exchanged letters with some of the people here today, but when I moved from Australia to Kenya our communications were cut off. So many of my friends, both men and women, whom I haven't seen for so long are all here together. I can't believe that Intisar gathered this many people to welcome me back. I feel as though I'm lost among them and don't know what to say. "The thing they remember the most are the love letters that we sent to that sociology professor at the university, my God, those days... we were happy despite the war," Rima says while we're hugging each other and laughing. "We were naughty!" I tell her. Jokingly she asks me, "Are you still?"

We'd drawn pictures in red pen of hearts and kisses, addressed the envelope to the sociology professor, with his office number in the Faculty of Arts and Sciences, and put it into the university's internal mail.

In the Rawda café I meet most of my friends, those friends, friends who have changed. Moments of silence pass between us and nothing can change this, except stories from the past, stories of a time we shared. I have to concentrate hard when they talk about politics, especially local politics. I concentrate so that I can follow the thread as they're talking to me. But I still don't understand everything.

Intisar says, "In this country you'll find different groups. There are people who talk about the war like it happened in another country. Like they've forgotten everything. The past has become a story you read about in a book. There are some who've forgotten how people stood on their balconies applauding for young militia men while they dragged an unarmed man along the ground because he happened to be from a different sect. Some man they kidnapped at a flying roadblock or a checkpoint. Of course they say that the war's over, but perhaps nothing is over. There's a place for everyone: for the person who wants to forget and the person who wants to remember. What's important is to know where you want to position yourself." Intisar says all this while looking at my face, wide-eyed. It's as though she's pointing her finger at me, accusing me of committing a crime, though I don't know what. Maybe it's the crime of having a memory, especially the memory of those who left the country during the war. It's as if someone who emigrated has no right to remember—to remember violence, to remember the war. The war's not over, I say to myself, while Intisar continues, as though delivering a speech prepared in advance. Stories about the war go nowhere but backward; they return to the same place they started from and then sometimes flare up, taking on a more violent form.

History repeats itself. Is this because of the nature of the place? Is it because of the terraces that are peculiar to the land here? Our history comes like our land... cut off, broken, incomplete, re-making itself in repetitive rows. Is this because our cities die and can't find anyone to bury them? Why here, in this particular spot in the world, is violence reborn hundreds of times?

Here, in the midst of friends, conversations, shouting, then silence, I imagine that I'm playing out my losses. This is all I have in Beirut.

Rima, who's getting ready to open a restaurant downtown, starts talking to Intisar, saying that the war's over. I pay little attention. Words derive their credibility from the person who utters them; they have no power outside this. They become merely voices, like wind echoing in the forest. A relative of Rima's who's come back from the Gulf rented a recently renovated old building in order to open a chain of restaurants and has put Rima in charge of managing one of them. Wonderful! Intisar pronounces.

Everything happens here as though life is normal, though there are still roadblocks and checkpoints in many places. People in Beirut do whatever they please, but in order to stomach this, they eat nostalgia with a fork and knife and then broadcast the leftovers through the media. Old Beirut is transforming into rubble with skyscrapers on top of it, with restaurants, amusement parks and religious buildings. Wafaa bends toward me as though she wants to share some kind of secret, saying that she—like me—doesn't understand what's going on.

"I keep trying to understand what's going on, and it's torture," she says.

"Checkpoints are still all over the place, nothing's right. It still isn't calm but—they say the war's over! I don't understand, that's why I'm doing yoga," Wafaa says, bitterly sarcastic. When I say I'd like to try a yoga class with her, we arrange to go together in the coming week.

"Don't try to understand, concentrate on your yoga lessons, dear, that's better!" Unfortunately, Intisar has overheard her and chimes in passive-aggressively. She goes on, "You too?! As if it's not bad enough with Myriam! But Myriam's been out of the country... You, what's your excuse for not understanding? You can't link two things together... roadblocks and sandbags are still there... what does this mean? Do you want to say that things haven't calmed down yet, but the war's over? OK. Just accept that this is what happens here: the war stops, tourists come back, and the sandbags are still there at the checkpoints!"

Intisar raises her voice, then calms back down, "Maybe it's better to see every event independently from the one before it. One event has nothing to do with the next. Then we can deal better with what's happening. It's easier, less painful."

"Yellah, my wife's scene is over," Malek says theatrically, announcing the end of Intisar's speech. "Yes, the scene's over, but I haven't finished yet!" Intisar answers, directing her statement at me. Despite their differences, when Intisar speaks she reminds me of Seetajeet, my psychotherapist in Mombasa. Maybe because they're similar in their confidence that what they're saying is the absolute truth: a truth which, for me, is never stable or at all self-evident. The war's stopped and there are still piles of sandbags. I must accept this; I must stop trying to understand. I'll learn how, I tell myself. There's no doubt that it would be very hard to follow the progression of events from the outside, from far away, seeing each event as independent and having no past, no relationship to what came before. But it's not impossible. It's inconsistent with the concept of history, but it's good to try, even if only once in my whole life! "We don't have choices here. We only have one thing, that's it, forgetting!" Wafaa says as I put out my last cigarette in the already full ashtray.

But what about those people who fought the war... who killed and kidnapped and mutilated bodies... Where are they? And where are their victims?

The waiter comes with a pot of tea and plates filled with manaqeesh, labneh and vegetables. Instisar calls out to him to come back and asks for "country-style" olive oil, as she calls it. "Country-style olive oil, please, from the Koura... Yes!" Then she turns to me saying, "The difference between you and us dear is that we lived devastation daily. It's over ... we've gotten used to it. Soon you'll get used to everything, believe me." She says this while cutting pieces from the big tomato and distributing them to everyone seated around the table. Then she turns toward Wafaa and asks her about her husband's health, because she'd hinted at a setback he suffered after emergency heart surgery.

"Are you back in Lebanon for good?" Wafaa asks me. Her question takes me by surprise and I don't know how to answer. I shake my head left and right, to indicate I don't know yet. Afterward I remain silent. She follows up, "Look for somewhere else, you won't be able to live here. Life here is disgusting, as you can see. The country's divided between killers and killers. We're only hostages, it's just disgusting!"

As Wafaa says these final words, she tilts her head toward Intisar, indicating a secret link between Intisar's words and what's disgusting. Or perhaps simply between what's disgusting and Intisar herself. There was always tension between Intisar and Wafaa, from our university days until now. Perhaps this can be traced back to the secret, short-lived relationship between Intisar and Wafaa's married brother. When Wafaa found out, it was a major catastrophe. Once Wafaa had invited Intisar home. By chance, she'd introduced her to her brother and what happened, happened. Intisar started skipping meetings and appointments with her girl friends. For Wafaa this was tantamount to treason.

Malek is still exactly how he always was. He talks about big dreams, as distant as a rainbow, as Intisar says. He confuses me. I never know when he's joking and when he's serious. He's always sitting on the fence: he defends the resistance and at the same time says Lebanon must remain a unique country within the larger Arab region.

In the past, he used to sometimes say that the Palestinians destroyed the country. But he also says that they're the last resistance movement in the world and we must support their revolution. He likes to talk about his hope that we can fix the country, get rid of sectarianism, and other big dreams that won't work for a country like Lebanon. We start talking about the importance of the role of the Shi'a as an avant-garde sect to create an alternative culture in the country.

"Stick to your dreams and you'll change the world for sure!" Intisar says without looking at him, as though he were incurable, a hopeless case.

"What... now it's forbidden to dream, too?!" Malek shouts. "I thought that dreams could change the world, but they always end in dictatorships. We still have to dream, though!"

"What's important is that we talk about something practical," Intisar says.

"You want something practical?" Malek asks, "What are we doing to stop killing each other? Please respond. This is an example of a practical question."

"We must learn to manage our civil wars," I answer sarcastically. "We need to create a state-run general directorate called the Department of Civil War Management, a department for the public good."

"Indeed, that would be a department for the public good," Rima comments.

How much more hopeful can you get? Bloody fighting is a way of life here. It's a kind of consumption, like alcohol, smoking, pop music and advertising on TV. There's civil war and then there's Gemmayzeh... and Downtown, Monot Street, Hamra, Jounieh, Maameltein and Ras Beirut... There's everything. Things that never meet and that have nothing to do with each other. But although they never meet, they feed off of each other, I think.

I leave the Rawda café and walk toward the hill leading up from the Hammam al-Askari. I leave my friends—the long conversations and shouting and unending disagreements going nowhere—behind me. The sun starts to set slowly into the sea, bidding me farewell as I walk up toward the AUB neighborhood. Motorbikes crisscross the streets, behind me, in front of me, and right near me, roaring like wild animals.

Suddenly one comes up right behind me, flying fast into and then over a stopped car and falling hard to the ground. Its driver lands on top of it. His body falls to the ground and his bike is turned upside down, its motor still running. The driver of a second motorbike starts shouting right in my face, stopping his bike to say that I'm the reason for this accident. It wouldn't have happened if I hadn't been walking in the middle of the street. He says that the driver tried to avoid crashing into me and so instead crashed into the car stopped in front of him. People gather as the wounded driver stands up and shakes off the dust and dirt from his clothes, paying no attention to the blood streaming from his head. He looks at me as though I'm a criminal who's gotten off easily, and curses and swears. Much of his cursing is directed at my mother.

I go back to my flat on Makhoul Street at sunset. I know that another day's passed in God's world and that this country will see more days live and die. The god who lives on top of the world can no longer hear, so when our screams reach him they're nothing more than feeble musical notes.

I'm here all alone after the difficult meeting with friends from my past. How can I adapt to this Beirut—the new-old Beirut which hasn't changed, but which I no longer know? Beirut hasn't changed, but it has lost its soul.

I fall asleep and then wake feeling as if I hadn't slept at all. For many years I've only been able to sleep for one cycle. They say that a person can't wake up energized and face the day peacefully if she hasn't slept for two full cycles, that is to say eight hours. I sleep one cycle. When I wake up, I think that I should go back to sleep but I can't. My mind is racing with a list of things that I have to do.

My continual exhaustion accompanies me as I start my day. The difference is that now I'm used to these feelings, as if exhaustion is part of me, not something unexpected that I have to get rid of. It's natural to pass my days with red-rimmed eyes. Sleeping more than four hours a night is unnatural for me. The pain in my legs and feet is part of my exhaustion.

I have come to believe that pain is a condition of existence for certain bodies. To live in our bodies means to experience pain. I've also started to believe that feelings are like this too—always mixed with pain, with bodily suffering. But I can't stay relaxed with the first threads of dawn. I hear the ticking of the clock that hangs on the wall of the furnished apartment I'm renting and which I think of getting rid of every day.

I get out of bed and go to the balcony that faces AUB. In the past, I used to listen to the ringing of the clock on College Hall, before the building was intentionally destroyed by an attack a few years ago. I no longer see the tower between the walls of the buildings in front of me. Almost nothing remains of the memory of the three years I spent at this university. Despite this, my heart remains open.

The light that creeps in from behind the sky doesn't lift the thin veil of darkness from the face of the earth. Indeed this light makes me more fearful—the muscles of my face and body tense. I try to go back to sleep but I can't. Faces of everyone I've seen since I've been back run through my mind. Full lips, youthful faces, tight skin, sleeplessness, drinks, eyes extinguished and desperately sad.

I can't sleep, but nonetheless I go outside to contemplate the sunrise at dawn. I haven't witnessed the birth of Beirut's sun for a long time.

I return to Beirut feeling like I've endured my forced exile like I endure hiccups—hiccups that are constantly with me and have become part of my life.

I leave my apartment and head up to Hamra Street. I'm there before the shop owners who haven't yet started their days. Hamra Street has changed. Even the women walking down it have changed. Their legs are still hidden inside black stockings, though it's the height of spring. Can they really not feel the weather? Or does death inhabit the women of Beirut, wrapping itself up in black clothes?

In the first part of the yoga class I have to get used to concentrating on my extremities. I begin by concentrating on the tip of my nose, so I close my eyes and start to relax. I can't relax while concentrating at the same time. I discover that it's easiest to concentrate on the furthest point of my extremities. I concentrate on the big toe of my right foot. Without meaning to, I move to my left. I think, I relax, I stop thinking. I breathe air into my lungs and keep it inside as long as possible. I feel the oxygen penetrating my veins with profound difficulty, as though cement walls impede its path. Little twinges grip me whenever the air penetrates more deeply. As though these twinges are the result of the edges of my soul crashing against my body on the inside. I can't do any more.

I leave the yoga class and walk from Hamra Street to Dr. Adam's clinic, the doctor who performed my abortion in the fall of 1979. His clinic is closed. I ask about him and they tell me that he was killed during the last years of the war.

I lost my child long ago. I was twenty-one and Georges was about the same age, or rather he was five years older but I never used to feel our age difference. I discovered my body with him and, although he had some experience, he discovered his masculinity with me. We discovered our bodies and our desires completely, once… twice … three times.

A year into our relationship, I found out I was pregnant and that I had to get rid of the pregnancy. He took me to a doctor, who he said was a relative of his. A

well-known doctor who had a big private clinic in Ras
Beirut. The doctor was handsome, though to me his good
looks seemed too perfect and somehow suspicious. Two
days later, I returned to the clinic alone and stayed there
for a day and a night. I left in the morning, alone, since
Georges didn't come to pick me up.

I left alone, while the cells of my baby, who never
became a fact, stayed in a big bin in the operating room.
I didn't ask anything: I never saw the doctor again. But
from the moment I left, I decided to keep my distance
from the man who had shared the discovery of my body,
who shared my pleasure. He didn't come to the clinic with
me and didn't come to pick me up when I left. At that
moment, it was like I was the only one who was guilty. He
was simply not there. He didn't lie down on the cold bed,
his arm wasn't pricked by the needle, and the old spinster
nurse didn't look at him with cold, glassy eyes and ask
him, contemptuously and with open hatred, if his family
knew about this. This wasn't his experience; it's my
experience alone. He didn't share it with me at all, ever.
I decided to distance myself from him, but this isn't
exactly what happened. I could only keep him out of my
life for a short period. Then I went back to waiting for him
and loving him.

Now that I have returned from Mombasa, I want to
visit the doctor. I want to complain to him about my
inability to conceive. Perhaps I choose him specifically
because I need to hear that I'm fine, that I can conceive,
that this is a superficial, passing problem. Who better to
tell me this than the person who took the embryo out of

my tender, living uterus and threw it away? But he's no longer here. He was murdered.

I want to visit the places imprinted on my imagination and experience flashes of memories.' I've left a man behind me in Mombasa and returned to Beirut. I want to re-tell my story with Georges, not to make it live anew but to feel it flash through my body. But his story is lost, just as he is. Georges didn't follow me and I could never mourn openly. I could never mourn and so couldn't heal. How could I mourn him when he wasn't my husband or brother or father or at least fiancé? He was the father of a baby who was never born. He was just my lover. When a lover dies we bury our sadness with him and can never show it in public.

I have left a man in Kenya and I want to reclaim my story from him, but stories can't be reclaimed. I have to discover the rest of my story with Georges, discover his story and why he disappeared. Which story do I begin with, when they're all my stories? I return for all this, but I don't know that every return is a disappearance, because the past never returns. A return is only another sign of absence.

But what do I have to do to excavate my life, like a gravedigger who isn't yet convinced that the dead won't return?

I also came to take possession of the keys to my house, the one that my father inherited from his father, the keys to a house that has no gates. The house in Zuqaq al-Blat has five entrances, whose gates my grandfather painted different colors: green, yellow, brown and blue. All of them open onto a courtyard that from the entrance of the house appears walled in, though it's only a little bigger than a crescent. We inherited the house from my grandfather Hamza. My old grandfather, whom I only remember from a picture that shows him as tall, with a cane and tarboush. I was very young when he passed away. From Nahil's stories, I've invented a roaring voice for him and I've imagined us hiding from him at the end of the hallway when he came home. I've imagined the sound of the keys to the house ringing in my ears.

Nahil says that no one but Hamza could carry the keys; they were attached to his wide cloth belt, which changed into a leather belt a few years before he died. Salama never dared ask his father for the keys. After Hamza died, Salama inherited the house and its five keys. The first thing he did was to open up all the gates, asking Nadia to leave them open for the three days people came to the house to offer their condolences, to shake hands and console the family with a few words, then leave.

Salama went mad after our house was bombed. A small piece of shrapnel the size of a lentil, as the doctor describes it, drove him mad. It entered his brain and remains lodged there. We were all saved but Baha', who was on the balcony at the time, and never came back. I try to recall that night, the voices and fighting and the decisive announcement that we should leave the house and go down to the ground floor. But then my mother decided that we should stay where we are. I don't know why all of a sudden she decided that we'd stay home that night. Oh, if only my mother had known that my father would go mad and my brother would be killed.

The people who occupied the house after we left for the mountains used only one door. The other four stayed locked. Those strong iron locks, which neither bombs nor bullets could destroy, rusted. The residents made an opening in the wall and used that as the main entrance because it protected them from the bombs that came both from East Beirut and the city center.

I wonder why houses aren't for temporary use, like lives are. When I was a child my grandmother used to tell me how my grandfather brought many large door lintels to the house, each decorated with words like talismans. He brought men to carve sentences on the columns, which rested above the doors horizontally, sentences that I couldn't understand back then.

He also built a big room and put a giant stone fireplace in one of its corners. Nahil says that once when I was a little girl and Hamza was sitting with some guests, proudly reading them the words that he'd had carved on the house's columns and walls, I went up to him to ask, "Why go to all this effort, jiddo? You'll die soon and the house will be all alone. Why didn't you build a house that's your same age and will die when you do?"

Nahil says that my grandfather Hamza was perplexed; he didn't respond but called her over to tell her what I'd said. Perhaps Hamza couldn't believe that I'd asked such a question. He constantly proclaimed that life required hard work and continual effort; to think otherwise would not to be tolerated. He inherited this work ethic from his mother, who attended an Anglican primary school in Damascus.

Salama was also raised like this, although he was a
Druze, which at the end of the day isn't so different from
Protestantism in terms of its work ethic. But he didn't
replicate his father's passion for hard work. Indeed, his
whole life, Hamza refused to support his projects and
criticized him constantly to Nahil, "Your son, what use is
he? He doesn't carry his own weight. He doesn't do
anything." Nahil intervened to defend her son, saying that
he did work and struggled hard in his work. Hamza would
shake his head, rejecting Nahil's claims, further alleging
that nothing useful could ever come of Salama's work and
repeating angrily, "He's a baker whose bread won't rise—
no matter what he does, his bread won't rise."

We build houses meant to last for centuries but we
live in them for only a few years. We make things to last,
perhaps only to forget our own impending death. Hamza
never wanted to die. As Nahil used to say, he kept fighting
right to the last moment of his life. He built and decorated
the house to fight against death. Most people do the same,
of course. Had Hamza been rich, perhaps he would have
decorated his house in gold instead of stone, so that then
his certain death would be more disturbing and resonate
more loudly.

Nour takes me to the mountain house where Olga and
Nahil live. I want him to spend the night, but he makes
his excuses. He says that he's traveling the next morning
to Amman and then, from there, to Baghdad. In the early
evening I stretch out on the sofa in the sitting room and

when I get up I realize that Olga's gone to sleep early. I've awoken from a strange dream. The next morning, I tell Olga about this dream. I dreamed of Nour, the man I met after I left Kenya, about Chris, my husband who waits for me in Mombasa, and about the late Georges, whom I haven't seen in more than sixteen years. I dream about these three while asleep in the sitting room. In the dream Georges put wood on the fire and told the other two the story of his life. I could see myself lying on the big sofa, listening, yawning, with a pleasant warm feeling—that these three men of mine were all friends and that I could love them all, each in his own way. I was no longer suffering because of the different experiences of love, the meaning and content of which varied with each man. In the dream I was warm and content; my whole life lay ahead of me, without interruption, like a wide-open plain that hides no secrets.

Leaning her head toward me with the warmth and collusion of a lover, Olga asks me about Nour. I tell her that he's just a friend.

"What? You're going to stay strong this time? Or will you get all romantic and stupid like you always do?" Olga says, "My darling, a woman has to be a whore to live with a man." I don't answer, but struggle to recall some of Olga's failed romantic adventures, which I'd witnessed as a teenager. I realize that Olga isn't speaking to me but to herself. She's speaking to the young woman she once was and who couldn't choose the right man for her life. It's as if she's finally discovered what she should have done in the past and wants another chance. But the past is the past; we don't get to correct our mistakes. Olga's words come too late, like a woman who discovers birth control only after she's already turned fifty.

I believe that Olga is a desirable woman, and not only because I first learned love with Olga when I was just a teenager. But I see her life as an ongoing loss of faith in love. It took a long time for Olga to lose her faith that love could cause miracles.

I haven't seen Nour for a week. He's still in Amman. Sometimes I contemplate his perpetual travel and his ever-present worry. He uses his time to research, collect stories and transcribe old newspapers that he's found in the AUB library. He wants to know everything: the history of his family and their properties, which he believes are still there and still rightfully belong to his grandmother, his mother's mother.

Today is the twelfth of January, 1996. I've been here for five months. It was this exact same day sixteen years ago that we left Lebanon. Our voyage that day wasn't easy. We had to drive to Damascus and fly from there to London and then onto Australia. It was snowing and just before we reached Dhour al-Baidar, we had to wait for a long time until we could pass through because of snowstorms. The long journey was hard for Salama and for Nadia, who decided after Baha''s death to resign from life—to resign from all responsibility and even from speaking. She no longer cares about Salama, neither his madness nor his perpetual anxiety.

She would look at him and then turn toward me, as though to say, "Enough… I'm done! I can't take it any more, now it's your turn." Nadia hadn't spoken since Baha' was killed. Perhaps she no longer had anything to say. Sometimes I believe that she decided to stop speaking; she came to this point through a conscious decision-making process and not as a result of shock. Perhaps the death of my brother made it easier simply to go silent. I know that my mother didn't love my father when they married; I know that her father forced her to marry Salama, after she'd been engaged to a man she loved. Nadia always thought that it was because she loved this man that her father forced her to leave him. I also know that Hamza had traveled to Hasbaya, my mother's village, to ask Nadia's father for her hand and that he had consented without Nadia's knowledge. A distant kinship between my mother and father's extended families meant they both took it for granted that this marriage would happen.

My grandmother Nahil says that Nadia fainted on her wedding night. That she fell ill from fear and because Salama wasn't patient with her. But the real reason that she passed out is that she couldn't be with the man she loved. She had to accept that the person on top of her on her wedding night was someone else—a man she didn't love; she didn't even like how he smelled. She had only seen this man a few times, but his smell alone was enough for her to recognize him. She came to know him from his scent. She knew when he was coming to visit her father before he crossed the threshold of the house, as if his scent had a voice she could hear from far away.

I only remember one sentence that the speaking Nadia used to repeat to us: she had only ever once loved one man and she lost this man on the day she married Salama.

Nadia was destroyed by Baha"s death. He was her son, so she died too. She died because she's no longer really alive. For me, the tragedy of Baha"s death is no more terrible than Nadia's silence. She remains silent while the kitten meows at her, wanting food. She goes into the kitchen to feed Pussycat, who walks behind her silently, as though they have a lasting understanding that her silence will never change.

My brother looked like my mother—his eyes, his skin color and the shape of his face were all like hers. He even inherited the big mole on his ear from her. His height and build, however, are like my father's. As for me, I inherited Nahil's face—her dark skin and her big, black eyes. I inherited my thin, well-proportioned build from my mother. Baha' was distinctly Nadia's son, as if he were a part of her body. My father, who never showed any emotion toward his son during his life, cried at his funeral and then went mad. Perhaps my father didn't lose his mind because of the shrapnel that pierced his skull and stayed lodged there, but because his son died before ever hearing one loving word from his father.

My silent mother. I see how silent she really is when my brother is killed. Should I have waited for my brother's death to protest against my mother's silence? Salama inherited the house from Hamza and if Baha' had lived he would have inherited it from Salama. Should I inherit

Nadia's silence? Especially now when, with Baha''s death, I'll inherit the house? But how can a woman who didn't learn how to speak from another woman inherit a house? Only now do I know how much I resemble Nadia. I needed to embark on my journey in order to know this. I actually resemble Nadia quite a lot. I wasn't aware of this resemblance before, not when I was with Georges, nor with Chris, nor even with my British-Indian therapist. I see it only when I pick up pen and paper and start to write. I begin writing everything I've been silent about for years.

"I won't feel pain after today," I wrote at the time. It's as if the pain inside me has been mummified. It's inescapable. It's like needing a lot of fresh air to live and trying to gulp it down because you can't survive with just thin gasps.

I call Nadia in Australia; I ask about Salama. She says a few words and then falls silent. When she starts speaking again, she speaks in English, a language she started to master only after arriving in Australia. She speaks for a long time. Her voice seems as though it's healed from a chronic illness. Here, cancer spreads through Olga's body, while there my mother's voice remains silent. Her original language is in exile. She now speaks only in another language.

Her effusive words on the phone make me think that my mother's silence was a cancer of the soul. Her silence is not silence so much as a fragmentation and failing of her original language. This is how I understand my mother's silence in Arabic. It's the silence of a fragmented, failing woman. I have dreamed about her a few times, and in my dreams she's a strong woman who takes on the world, riding a bicycle furiously down the open street. I remember this dream when I call her. It's as if my dream has become real.

She tells me about her work in Adelaide, about the new immigrants who are Baha"s age. She can finally speak of Baha'; she speaks of him in her new language. There's only hope and power in these words, no sadness. We cry together for the first time, my mother and I.

Hamza's words are tantamount to action; he writes on stone, carves words. I don't understand the sentences he engraves on the doors. Nadia doesn't understand them either. He says they're there to protect the house and family. He always repeats this to people at Thursday evening get-togethers. Writing makes Hamza even stronger than he was before. Words make my mother more silent. Perhaps this is why people believe that words are for men alone. Words and writing are for men, only men, women have no right to them.

Did Nadia's silence begin here—even before she was born? From the time that these sentences were carved in stone, never to be erased or disappear? Carved in Arabic, carved in stone, in the body. How can I destroy those words? How can I transform them, make them into my own writing, my mother's writing?

I find no one in the Zuqaq al-Blat neighborhood where our house is... I can't find anyone I used to know. Ankineh is no longer here, the Armenian woman whose house the fighters entered, beating her and her husband and stealing their rugs and artwork right before their eyes. At the time she didn't say anything, but simply let them plunder. Perhaps they'd satisfy themselves, as she said. "Jibreel's gang robbed my house and stole my rugs," she said over and over again. After Jibreel's son was killed by a car bomb in Beirut, Ankineh would say, "Honestly, I don't rejoice at other people's misfortunes, but look what happened to his son." Though the doorway was wide, they couldn't get the huge chandeliers out of the front door, so they took them out onto the balcony and threw them down from the second floor. Little pieces of crystal radiated everywhere like fragments of a shattered sun. One of the neighbors tried to stop them, saying that there's no use taking valuables if you're just going to throw them from the balcony and break them, then they won't be worth anything. In response, they picked him up and threw him off the balcony as well. The fall broke his leg.

The shopkeeper whose store was in the building where Ankineh used to live tells me that he's never heard of such a name, seeming amazed that there could be a woman named Ankineh. This shopkeeper is a child of the war; the list of names he knows is small and includes only names of those who belong to one sect, one religion.

Ankineh was a friend of my grandmother's and often went to visit her in the mountains, staying for weeks, especially during oppressive Beirut heat waves. "You didn't know how to do anything, we had to teach you," Ankineh always said whenever she saw Olga preparing macaroons, the dessert she's famous for. "You only knew how to make bread!" Ankineh's memories were always vivid and present, despite her age.

Every time I sat with her, I asked her to tell me the story of how she came to Lebanon after the massacres that weighed so heavily on the lives of most Armenians in Turkey. She came to Lebanon in 1921 when the whole world was getting itself back in order after the end of the First World War. Ankineh came to Lebanon with her parents when she was five years old.

Her family had wanted to make their way to Jerusalem because they had relatives there, but they stayed in Lebanon and became Lebanese. They left everything they had in Turkey. The Turkish army took everything they had carried with them when they left their house. Ankineh would always thank God that her father didn't take his family to Jerusalem because many of the Armenians who were in Palestine in 1948, during the first Arab–Israeli war, took refuge in Lebanon, including Ankineh's relatives, who came to live with them in their house. Few Armenians have stayed in Jerusalem—most have emigrated to America or Canada or are preparing to emigrate now.

The house in our neighborhood was the fifth house that Ankineh had lived in since she moved to Beirut. When she and her family first arrived in Lebanon they were settled near the big theater in the middle of Beirut. Then they moved to Corniche al-Mazraa, where her father opened a jewelry shop. Her father had worked as a jeweler in Konya, Turkey. When they left Turkey, he sewed the jewels into blankets and covered the children with them.

Ankineh's mother had adopted two Armenian children who lost their families so that she could bring them on the train and then the boat without risking arrest by the Turkish army. The adoption happened as quickly as that. She told them, "I'm your mother. If anyone asks you who you are, that's all you tell them." When they arrived in Marsin by train to take the boat to Lattakia and then Beirut, the Turkish army forbade them to take their blankets with them. They were forced to leave everything behind, including the jewels still hidden in the blankets. Some Armenians first took refuge in Beirut and then emigrated, "Because Beirut is very small," as Ankineh used to say. They preferred to move on to Chicago, New York or Montreal. "Beirut is very small," Ankineh would repeat, turning her closed hand and then opening it, on her lips and in her eyes the trace of a smile lost somewhere between pride and pity. She meant that her closed fist represented Beirut's size. The word "small" for her meant two things. First, that everyone here knows everyone so everyone sees her as a stranger, an immigrant, or "eemeegrant" as she pronounced it. Second, that Beirut wasn't enough of a trade and manufacturing capital for Armenian businessmen. Born and raised in Istanbul, they were used to a cosmopolitan life that Beirut couldn't offer, so they left for Western cities.

Perhaps Ankineh was one of the few who came to Lebanon after the massacres of Armenians in Turkey and stayed until the end of the twentieth century. She married an Armenian man sixteen years older than her and never had children. When she would tell the story of her flight from Turkey, she'd say that she heard that Istanbul, or "Constantinople" as she preferred to call it, burned ten times after she left. She believed that these fires were the work of God, vengeance on behalf of her and her family. "This my darling, is God's wrath," she would tell me in Armenian-accented, broken Arabic, but with great confidence—as if she'd completely mastered the Arabic language and didn't need to explain anything.

In the building across the way are people whose names and faces I don't know. They don't know me either. The houses have changed on the inside and the outside. Only one woman, Yvette, remains on the second floor of the building across from our house, though her brother left for Canada a year after we emigrated. "We no longer have a place here," Yvette used to say before I emigrated. When she sees me, she doesn't repeat what she used to say about wanting to leave Lebanon. Instead, she opens her mouth, confused, "Mimo, my darling, it's you! People leave and you… What did you come back for?!" She carries on, her smile a false reprimand, "Like someone who leaves on a pilgrimage just when everyone else is coming back!"

Behind the building, the orange and fig trees have dried up. Only one decrepit pomegranate tree is still standing. It's leaning slightly against the wall of a building that's marked with holes of many sizes. Yvette says that the young men in militias didn't leave one green branch in the whole neighborhood. During ceasefires they discharged their weapons into the roots of trees, splitting them open like the bodies of human beings. When there were no more trees left, they started in on the walls around them and sometimes on whatever pedestrians they could see in East Beirut.

Where are these disappeared people that Yvette is talking about? Where are they? Why don't they come out and say something? Why don't they tell me what happened? Where are the people who disappeared, who've been disappeared? How were they killed, if they were killed? Where are the people who perpetrated all of the war's massacres?

It's as if the earth has swallowed them up. As if the earth has swallowed the witnesses, the evidence and the perpetrators. "They are all still here," Yvette says, tormented. "But you won't know who they are. They've become something else. They have new faces and we're not allowed to remember or even remind them of their old faces."

It is as if there's no place here for someone who silently witnessed the death of Beirut. No place for someone fleeing from death in Beirut. No place for someone coming back to search for a lost memory. Beirut is a devastated threshold. How can I cross over it? How can I return when I'm constantly moving from one place to another?

Nour returns from Amman. It's early evening and I'm lying down reading a book. I guess I'd dozed off because I glance up at the clock above the door before I hear the doorbell ring and get up out of bed. When I open the door I see him standing there, leaning against the wall as if he's about to lose hope of ever seeing me again. He's brought me the bags of Dead Sea salt that I'd asked for. He tells me that he's calling off the search for his roots. He says this on the verge of tears. He seems defeated, having lost all hope of finding any members of his family who are still alive. No doubt he's discovered that it's dangerous to feel hope in Beirut and that his search is futile.

I'm still half asleep and feel troubled when we go out together. I wasn't prepared for him to come by or even to see him just like that, all of a sudden. I'm not prepared to listen to his frustration about the journey to search for his roots, which at this precise moment means nothing to me. I didn't even look in the mirror before I opened the door to him and only later realized how I must have looked when he first saw me. I have the feeling that he's betrayed me with this visit, as though he's forcibly entered a place intimate to me, one I don't want him to enter. We walk along the sea in the Manara neighborhood. He starts talking and I don't want to talk. Suddenly, as though to anger me, he tells me that I've inherited my mother's silence. My mother, whom he's never met in his life, whom he knows only from the stories I've told him. Then he asks me if I want to sit down at a nearby café, across the road from the Corniche, because it's starting to rain.

Nour wants to spend the night with me. He doesn't want to go home and spend the night alone after his discouraging visit to Amman. I give him a t-shirt to wear. It used to be Chris's and I often wear it to sleep because it's comfortable and its cotton is soft to the touch. It looks almost exactly the same on him as it looks on Chris because they're about the same size, though Nour is a little shorter. It doesn't matter to me that he's wearing a t-shirt that belongs to a man who even at this moment is still technically my husband. It all seems simple and self-evident.

"I want to go back to my country," he says, searching for a match to light my cigarette. He keeps repeating that he wants to go back to his country. The fool doesn't know—he doesn't know that I want to be his country.

Mere hours after he leaves my apartment I see him in the street and I don't believe this is the same Nour, the Nour who was in bed with me all night. He's walking sluggishly, with little confidence. He looks around him anxiously, a man who has lost hope. "Nour, hi!" I call out to him from the sidewalk on the other side of the street. He hears a voice but doesn't see me at first. A few seconds pass before he notices me. Then he turns toward me, his face showing only slight surprise. From far away and with too big a smile on his face he shouts, "*Oh hello! Is that you?*" Then, as if he wants to make up for the inappropriate sentence he's just uttered, one not suited to two people who just a few hours ago were in bed making love, he mouths to me silently, *you are my love...* He looks strange standing like that on the other side of the street.

I can't see his shadow. Moments pass and I'm still searching for his shadow behind him.

It's exactly midday. He is standing in front of me like the upright hands of a clock at midday. I think that everything we've done together in bed has brought us closer, that the sexual pleasure we shared brought us neither closer to God nor to hell. Perhaps we were somewhere between the two. The animal words we exchanged left behind an aggressive, thrilling heat. The effects of an action never end. Even now, I don't know quite how to describe the moments between us. It's as if what happens between us is a dream, something unreal. Moments that occur outside time can't return to memory.

We exchange words, which the two sides of the street interrupt, as if we're carrying something heavy between us and we don't know where to take it. This heavy thing wants each of us to be done with it. At that moment a strange feeling surrounds me. I feel that his words may reflect what's inside him, but they remain deep inside him. They stay inside and never come out into the open. These words are, "How heavy life is, how difficult life is to live."

I haven't found anything in Beirut, I think. I've found nothing but a companion on my journey of loss.

My brother was killed. Less than two years after his death we found a way to leave Lebanon. Many things happened between these two events. The first is that my grandmother Nahil tried to marry off her son Salama again. For the sake of the family name and inheritance and so that the house would "remain open and never be closed," as she always used to say.

Nahil had to find a way to put this that would convince Nadia to let Salama marry again. To remarry, my father would have to first divorce my mother. In our religion—despite the fact that for marriage, theoretically, we follow the Hanafi school of law—a man cannot be married to more than one woman at a time.

Nadia offered no resistance. She didn't leave the big house and return to her family's house, which had been closed up since my only maternal uncle, Yusuf, left for Australia. It's as if her husband's remarriage was no more than a game to her.

While my grandmother was still talking, trying to convince Nadia of all the reasons that this plan of hers was necessary, Nadia indicated with her hand that none of this made any difference to her. Perhaps my mother no longer wanted anything or anyone. She had transformed into a box made of flesh, totally closed in on itself and content that way, with no needs or desires. All she did was sit all day long on my brother's bed and stare at his many photographs.

She was satisfied by going back to the old books she had brought with her when she came to her new house after marrying my father. Salama and Nadia's divorce never happened, since my father remarried as a Sunni Muslim. This all happened at the speed of light. Nahil was compelled to go along with this solution to the problem, despite her Druze faith, which caused a huge uproar in the extended family, especially among the men.

Nahil brought a woman in her thirties from Jordan, where most of my grandmother's relatives have settled.

She was a widow who had lost her husband in 1970 during the troubles between the Palestinian fedayeen and the Jordanian army. They were married the day the bride arrived because Nahil was afraid that the woman would change her mind when she met my father in person and saw how sick he was. She had to pay off everyone at the court that day to get it all over with quickly. That's what she told Olga.

After the shaykh registered their marriage, she brought the bride back to the house, into the living room, holding her hand. She pointed to my father, who had entered the room before them and was standing and staring at the suitcase that his new wife had leaned against the sofa. She said, "Yellah, that's your husband. We want a boy in nine months!"

Nadia watched all of this happen. No one from the extended family came to witness the registering of Salama's marriage. Olga attended, as did the brother of the new wife, who accompanied her from Jordan, despite his obvious limp and leg pain, both of which made it necessary for him to remain seated.

None of the men of the family accepted what Nahil had done. They told her that she was "making decisions and doing whatever she wants" as though our family had no men in it.

They also said that Hamza never managed to discipline her, not even once, and maybe Salama went mad because of her, not because of the shrapnel in his head.

The women of the family said that this was a cursed day and that Nahil had sinned. They said that she shouldn't defy God's will—if our family had been destined to have a male heir who would carry on the family name, my brother wouldn't have died.

But Nahil didn't listen to any one of their opinions, that is to say she didn't listen at all. Instead, she put the couple in the bedroom and locked the door. Not one of the men of the family dared hold Nahil accountable for what she'd done, fearing that she'd use her curses—which always come true—against them.

In the bedroom, Salama didn't know what to do when this woman took off her clothes, pushed him onto the bed and rode him, saying, "Your mother wants a son and that's what I'm here for. Let's go!" The woman stayed with my father in the bedroom and no one saw them for three days, except in the minutes when they each used the bathroom.

Nahil sent Olga in with a tray of aphrodisiac foods: little dishes of mezzeh, raw meat and sweets. All the while she sat in the living room near the balcony and prayed, muttering words without a book.

Sometimes she prayed for Salama so that he'd be healed and get his right mind back. She prayed for Baha''s soul, Baha' whom she forcefully believes was born again in another place not far from her.

Sometimes she would open the Hikmeh and ask for God's forgiveness, saying that her many sins were the cause of Salama's misfortunes.

Nahil believes that her curses influence the destinies of people around her. That's what everyone around her believes, too. She prayed for Salama to conceive again, even though she believed that the curses she unleashed on Hamza in the past have done their job.

"May God deprive you of continuing your family name!" she told Hamza after learning that he'd betrayed her. She learned of his betrayal from his changed smell. "What's her story? She curses your grandfather to deprive him of his family name, and then when it happens like she wanted it to—then she wants to marry your father off so he can have another son?" Olga said to me in a soft voice. She objected to Nahil's behavior, but her objections remained confined to whispers and head shaking, in disbelief.

Neither Nahil's prayers nor Salama's seclusion with the woman resulted in anything. It was no use. The woman didn't get pregnant and Nahil waited for a whole year, sighing continually and repeating to everyone who could hear the proverb that she's famous for, "Blessings on the family that produces sons to secure the future of their family home." It's as if it took Baha''s death to make her suddenly realize that he was the sole heir and that his death meant the end of the family home forever.

Nahil isn't convinced that our family home doesn't have a male heir; she won't accept the fact that in the end I alone will inherit everything. Of course she knows that I haven't been blessed with a son from my marriage to Chris, and she doesn't know anything about the baby that was pulled out from inside me in Doctor Adam's clinic and thrown away before I left the country.

"My daughter, do you want the English to take our inheritance?" she asks me after I come back, when I'm trying to help Olga to get out of bed and walk a little, over to her wardrobe. By this, she means Chris and his children from his two previous marriages. She says this while advising me to register the house in the name of male relatives on my father's side. This is the very same predicament Nahil found herself in. The fact that the male heir she desires does not exist means that nothing prevents me from inheriting what's mine.

She opens the drawers of her wardrobe and takes out a bronze key ring with five keys on it. She also takes out documents and property deeds. She gives them to me, saying with great sadness that the Zuqaq al-Blat house has become my property now, after Salama's madness and the death of Baha', the only male heir. She's still waiting for Salama to come back, when I tell her about his situation in Australia she says that I'm complicating matters and exaggerating his mental state. No doubt he'll be cured when he returns. Doctors here are better, she says, as soon as his feet touch the ground in the airport he'll feel better.

Nahil doesn't ask me what I'll do—if I even want this inheritance or if it means anything to me. Of course it doesn't cross her mind to bring me a man, as she did with my father, to marry him to me so that I could be blessed with a son to carry on the family name and family home. But this wouldn't happen even if I produced one thousand sons. My son won't carry my name. Indeed, my name will be lost to him from the very beginning, as I lost it myself after I married. Many years separate me from Nahil, of course, but in our two different times the issue of the name and the inheritance remains the same. A young woman still leaves her family home to go to her husband's home and family all alone, denuded of everything, even her name. Thus, you must pass on an inheritance to a male heir. The child must be a boy. A girl is useless, even one hundred girls. This is not only true today, but throughout time. Why is Nahil so concerned about a male heir? Isn't she a woman? How could a woman agree to her own burial when she's still alive?

Nahil's contradictory qualities perplex me, though I guard a giant love for her deep in my heart. Wasn't it she who taught all the girls in the village how to read and write, when she was a young woman teaching in the French girls' school? To achieve all her aims in this closed society, she came up with a clever strategy, in which it was easier for a father to say his daughter was dead than that she was learning how to read and write.

She opened a sewing school, though she'd never held a needle and thread in her life. She said that she wanted to teach the girls in the village about housekeeping and the domestic arts. At the time, being able to sew was one of the qualities that made a girl a sought-after bride. Nahil committed herself to sewing, convinced this was her calling, and asked to teach the girls for two hours a day in her parents' house. She devoted the big salon with its view of the main road to her sewing lessons.

The families went crazy when one day she asked the girls to bring chalkboards to write on. They visited Nahil's father in protest and asked him if she was teaching their daughters to read and write. Her father called her in to ask her and she entered the room and greeted the girls' families, inquiring after their crops and their relatives. She invited them to stay a little longer and offered them sweets she had prepared herself.

She told them that she was teaching their daughters the letters related to sewing, cutting garments, and housekeeping, only because these were necessary. As for the letters related to love and to rejecting customs and traditions, "That's monstrous—of course not!" She told them that she was like them and that, like them, she would never sanction educating their daughters!

She's a strong woman. Despite this strength, her husband Hamza managed to keep his relationship with a woman from Zahleh secret from her for more than thirty years. When Hamza died, Nahil forgot everything bad about him. She mourned him, cried over his corpse, and asked for forgiveness for him. The truth disappeared at the moment of his death. It's as if the truth had been erased; at that moment it became absent, as if it had never been. When I try to remind her of aspects of Hamza and his love stories that she did and didn't know, she starts repeating, "Oh, Abu Ibrahim… Oh, Abu Ibrahim, what's all this talk?" trying to get up from her chair, which each year seems bigger and bigger compared to her emaciated body.

That she has magic powers doesn't mean that she knew about Hamza's movements. He would tell her that he went to Soufar to store up ice to sell in the summer to merchants and passengers on the train between Beirut and Damascus who stop in the 'Ayn Soufar station. After refrigerators became widespread, there was no more selling ice in Soufar; soon the train stopped running and the station disappeared. But Hamza kept on saying that he worked there and Nahil kept up the appearance of believing him. After his death, she found many letters among his papers, as well as verses and love poems that perhaps he had intended to send to the woman he loved. But this all remains in his leather suitcase, preserved with care in the wooden cupboard above the door. This life of his didn't prevent Nahil from going, after his death, to a photography studio to have color added to his photo before she hung it on the wall.

The day we left for Australia, Hamza's colored photograph was still hanging in the living room. By talking about him, Nahil keeps his presence in the house strong. Sometimes I think that she's making Hamza into a fairytale hero—a man everyone fears, especially my father. Nahil makes sure he's ever-present in the house; she always recounts stories about him and keeps his portrait hanging in the living room.

After his death, Nahil took the original black-and-white portrait to Harut, the photographer, near our house in Zuqaq al-Blat, and asked him to color it.

At first Harut was perplexed by Nahil's request. He told her that men never ask to change the color of their photographs, only women do. Nahil insisted, almost losing her patience, "Hamza entrusted it to me and died, how can you know what he would have wanted?" She took Hamza's small cloth wallet out of her bag and gave all the money in it to Harut, saying, "If you don't know how to color it, I'll take it to Vicken." Vicken was the owner of a studio near AUB.

She didn't want Harut to choose only the colors he wanted for Hamza; she wanted all the colors. She stood in front of him with the picture in her hand and described the color of the shirt that Hamza was wearing in the portrait, the color of his trousers and his tarboush, though they all appeared to be the same color. She wanted to be sure of everything before she left the studio. Every time he made a colored photograph and took it from the black box behind the curtain, she would shake her head disapprovingly and ask him to redo it. Harut colored my grandfather's cheeks red, and his lips too, so he looked like a clown dressed up in a fighter's clothes. In black-and-white, the weapon Hamza bears looked frightening; in the new photo it looks like it's made of plastic, the kind of toy children use to play war.

The male line in our house ended with my brother's death. Nahil's repeated complaint was no use—she wanted more sons for my father, but my mother Nadia refused to have more than two children: my brother Baha' and me. She was afraid that another pregnancy would end in the baby's death and so she refused to have a big family. She has carried this fear with her from her own childhood; it's a fear she's been living out from the first time she gave birth and it predates even her marriage to Salama.

Nadia is the only survivor in a family whose mother bore more than five sons, each of whom died at birth. Every time my grandmother, Nadia's mother, gave birth, the baby died the moment he was born or a few days afterward. Not only did this mother suffer through the pains of pregnancy and childbirth, she then had to suffer the loss of her baby. This was enough to make her accept her husband's accusations that she had rolled over onto the baby while she was sleeping and killed it.

Nadia was the only one who lived, despite her soft, delicate constitution. When Nadia was a small child, they took her to a shaykh in the Biqaa who was meant to help her mother bring boys into the world who would survive. They took her first to visit the Prophet Job's shrine and fed her sweets and fruit. Then she got back in the car and was taken to a place near the house of the shaykh where he sat her in a big basket. The weather was cold and the basket had a long rope tied to it so it could be lowered into a dried-up well. Nadia was small and from the opening of the well she looked like a bundle of folded clothes forgotten in the basket.

When the basket reached the bottom of the well, the shaykh asked her to wish aloud for whatever she desired, and then, by God, all her wishes would come true. They had told her at home to ask for a brother and not to ask for toys or sweets or clothes. Everyone prepared her in advance to say the right words. "Ask for a brother, called Yusuf," they told her, repeating it over and over again so that she'd memorize the name. The shaykh repeated his question, "What do you want?"

She couldn't speak. She couldn't answer, because she had started to think: What if she asked God to bring her a brother and then he died after he was born like the other baby brothers? What if her mother got pregnant again with another baby who was born and then died? And then another baby was born and died? She could see her mother's face, her mother's body rolling on the floor, moaning in pain. She could hear her crying. Suddenly she heard the shaykh's voice descending toward her from the opening of the well. When she didn't answer, the voice began to shout. She started to shiver, her teeth chattering from cold and fear. But she didn't ask for anything, she stayed silent. The shaykh yelled louder. At the time, it felt as if it was her father screaming down at her. They seemed to have the same voice. Suddenly she raised her voice— soft, weak and frightened—from the bottom of the well. Her words were like a wail. Hesitant and fearful, she asked for only one thing. She asked God to make her father die and free her mother from him. Then she lost herself in disjointed, strangulated sobs.

When my mother's only brother Yusuf was born, my maternal grandmother dressed him in little girls' clothes for four years. She said this was the only way to keep the evil eye far from him.

My grandmother Nahil has died. I went into her room one morning and thought she was still sleeping.

I go to see Nour three days after I lose my grandmother Nahil. I want to see him, to see his face and eyes, to know that everything's well with him. When I see him I relax. We walk together from his office to his house, a short distance that seems to take a lifetime.

When we arrive, he locks the door behind him. At that moment I understand the meaning of the expression "Your heart is shattering in your palm." My heart plunges.

I don't know what to do when I enter. I pick up the jacket that I had put on the back of the sofa when I walked in and put it on. I do exactly the opposite of what is usually done. What we'd wear to go out, I put on as we enter. It's as if I'm hiding the passion bursting from inside me, preserving it, fearing it, pushing it back inside one more time—with my clothes. But as soon as I've put on the jacket I discover that nothing in the world, absolutely nothing, can keep my desire from escaping. I leave my arms around him. I leave my head, its sadness and desire, on his shoulders. I bury my face in the folds of his wine-colored sweater. I need to breathe in his scent. It enters my pores like an act of love. A force pushes me toward him. I forget my house in Kenya; I forget what brought me here to Lebanon; I forget everyone in the world. I want only him at this moment, powerfully. I want to be with him alone. The two of us alone together with the door locked behind us. I shut the door firmly. I leave the world outside.

I come close to him. He is familiar and friendly. His scent—the scent and fragrance of his skin—penetrates my every pore. He says that he's nervous and afraid. I don't say anything. He says that with every human death a little bit of God dies, that love and death can't encounter each other, that he doesn't like making love at moments like these. I don't understand what he's trying to say. I know only one thing: that during Nahil's burial, a passion and desire for him swept me away. A vague force pushed me toward him as though nothing within me could resist death except a moment of love with him. My hands journey across his body, to discover him through touch.

He seems lost and anxious… His kisses were that way too, they slid from my face to my neck and my chest to my belly then my vulva. He's quick and absentminded, his mouth doesn't pause. I want him to come inside me, quickly. I feel that he's bringing a deep pain out from inside me, a pain that resides there and has become part of my body. I hear myself moaning, my sighs increasing like the echo of a wounded animal in a forest. Then I start to cry. I couldn't cry the day Nahil died. Only now can I cry for her. I start crying with Nour, who seems like a child, in how hard he's trying to satisfy me.

On the night before her death, Nahil called for Olga and asked her to help her take a shower. When Olga tried to put the shower off until morning, she got agitated and screamed at her. Olga bathed her and poured water infused by bay leaves on her damp hair and rosewater all over her body. When Olga wrapped her in a big towel, Nahil took her hand and asked her to help her get to her bed.

The old woman seemed exhausted and couldn't walk. When she got to her bed she seemed refreshed and asked Olga to sit near her. She took Olga's hand, drew it to her again, then put it between her thighs, saying, "Look… it's like I'm still a young woman." When Olga tried to move away, Nahil pressed her hand and asked, "You've been with a man, of course?" Olga withdrew her hand and started to lift the towel off of her to help her put on her nightgown and said, impatient and exhausted because of her illness, "No!"

"You haven't experienced a man's liquid?" Nahil asked.

"No... It's better this way," Olga answered.

"This was the first time she'd started to lose her mind." This is what Olga told me, her face betraying an unspoken anxiety for Nahil.

The next day, Nahil didn't wake up. She was stretched out on her bed as though asleep.

I see Olga fading away and I can't say anything. I'm not ready for another loss. This is too much for one year.

Shortly before my return to Lebanon, Intisar sent me a report from Olga's doctor so I could show it to a British doctor who's a friend of my husband's. The doctor had told her that she should begin chemotherapy, but Olga refuses to submit to this kind of treatment. On the phone I asked Intisar to check up on Olga and see how she's doing. I've never had the courage to bring up the subject of her cancer with her, as though bad news will get better, or less harsh, if it passes through other people's mouths before it reaches me.

It's hard for her to accept her emaciation and the changes in her appearance. But the Olga that I know and love endures, as does her perpetual movement, its remnants overcoming her atrophying body and yellowing face.

In my early adolescence, we slept in the same bed. She reached out to touch my body. She taught me pleasure. She kissed me on my mouth and then asked me to kiss her as she kissed me. In my first relationship with a boy, who was only a year older than me, I relied on the sexual knowledge that Olga had passed on to me. She was the one who supplied me with my first instructions. The discovery that men had different parts than Olga and I did was a surprise. We took off our underclothes before sleeping, as she'd learned to do in her convent boarding school, run by French-speaking Swiss nuns. Then she would tell me about her mad grandmother, who was a bad cook and boiled everything in salt water. She told me she'd never had herbs or spices until she moved in with Nahil after her grandmother's death, when she hadn't yet reached seven years of age.

In bed, Olga repeated the story of her birth and the death of her mother Myriam, after whom I'd been named by my grandmother Nahil—even though my mother had chosen another name, Asmahan. Olga told the story of how her grandmother had raised her and how, when her grandmother was dying, she asked my grandmother Nahil to take her in, although the family disapproved of a Druze woman adopting a Christian girl. As was her habit, my stubborn grandmother didn't listen to anyone. She took Olga in, Olga who had no parents, and sent her to the convent boarding school to study just like the other Christian girls in the area.

The reason my grandmother agreed to care for Olga and educate her like her own daughter, despite the difference in age and sect between them, goes back to a story dating seven years before I was born, a story exactly the same age as Olga herself. While Myriam was at home giving birth to her daughter Olga, my father's sister, who had been born with an incomplete, deformed heart, was struggling, taking her dying breaths in the hospital. My grandmother was in the hospital room beside her daughter, facing the doctor, who advised her to take her daughter home so she could die in her own bed, in peace among her family. The young woman lost consciousness and everyone thought that she had died, but a few moments later she awoke, saying that she'd just seen her mother giving birth to her not far from her family's house. She saw herself as an infant trying to escape a narrow, dark tunnel. She saw herself for a few moments in the darkness of the womb.

"Hurry up, make me beautiful, dress me, my mother's giving birth to me! My mother's giving birth to me, the cross around her neck is dripping sweat," my young aunt said feebly. Then she stopped moving and fell silent. It wasn't hard for anyone there to guess the identity of the girl born at the exact moment my aunt died. My aunt died while Myriam was giving birth to a little girl at home, beside her the midwife who had come especially from Aley to help her. Myriam herself died only one day after giving birth to her beautiful baby girl. They said that her placenta, which refused to come out, poisoned her. The baby carried her name from the moment of her birth. While she was losing consciousness, her mother called her Olga. Everyone who believes in the transmigration of souls believes that when my aunt died she was newly reborn.

Olga cries every time incense is burned. When I ask her why she cries she tells me that the smell hurts her heart. She believes the smell pains her to the point of death and that Nahil told her how she discovered Hamza's betrayal from the changed smell of his skin and breath whenever he came home after being away. Nahil told her that she knew about his betrayal from the beginning, but she chose never to bring up the issue with him. Every time he came back from seeing the other woman, she would ask him about his work selling ice. She told him that the trade in ice was a losing proposition and that he needed to change his business.

The hospital waiting room is drowning in sick people and there's only one empty seat, right beside an enormous ashtray filled with cigarette butts. I offer the seat to Olga and stand next to her, waiting for our turn. I know what the doctor will say. I know there's no magic cure for Olga's illness except in fairy tales. But I wait to hear what the doctor will say. I wait for him, looking past him at the x-ray he's busy hanging on a transparent white board that emits light.

"I haven't visited Dhour al-Choueir for years," Olga says with something like hope. "There's an old hotel, an old house whose owners turned it into a hotel. Take me there. I want us to go there together on the weekend."

Olga and I never ever speak about our relationship— things happen between us spontaneously, without words. I've learned how a woman takes off her clothes in front of another person. I have always felt, in the depths of my heart, that my relationship with her was a temporary way station, as I waited for another experience that would be more real. When I told her this, she laughed and hugged me. I waited for her to tell me that what I was living with her would be the most real thing in my life. But she didn't say anything. Her smile betrayed a certain compassion for a younger girl that always left me uncertain. Many years have passed and I can still taste Olga's skin on my lips.

That's magic, right? Magic, by God! She tells me flamboyantly, describing the aromas of the dishes she loves that fill the house. With her left hand she lifts the cover of the pot on the fire and with her right hand she stirs what's boiling in the pot. She sprinkles in the spices she likes, then lifts the spoon to her lips and tastes the food. "Oh mama, how delicious," she says. She'll cover the pot and start to sing. She'll look at me and say, "Your eyes are still just like they were when you were small. Your eyes were always full of questions. It's as if they devour the answers, every word, every motion, whether coming from a human or an animal. They're never satisfied, like open lips thirsty for a sip of water."

I put Olga's latest test results on the bottom of the suitcase. I put all the doctor's papers at the bottom of the suitcase and zip it closed as though I don't want to remember and don't see any other solution. Olga sleeps on the way to Dhour al-Choueir. Her body seems small, like the body of a teenage girl. Her hair has thinned. She's weak and debilitated.

In the hotel room, she takes off her clothes, one article at a time, and appears to be shaking. I go to her to help her get in bed. The air is warm and the windows are all the way open. There's absolutely no air circulation; the curtains are motionless. I draw back the bedcovers and clear a place for her to sleep. She keeps holding my hand for a few moments and pulls me gently toward her. With a kindly gesture, she motions to me to sit with her in bed. She closes her eyes. I take off some of my clothes and throw them on my bed by the window. I stand for a moment, then turn and see Olga looking at me. I take off my remaining clothes and walk naked toward her bed. I lift the covers on the other side and slip in beside her, with the intimacy of two people whose relationship has not dissipated because of distance.

She turns to me, I notice a weak half-smile on her face, and I encircle her with my arms. Her naked body is very cold, despite the hot weather. Her skin is smooth but dry. As I draw nearer to her I feel heat creeping through her body. She buries her delicate face in my naked breasts. Time passes like this before our breathing together takes on an even, harmonious rhythm. I pass my hand over her back as though I'm getting to know her all over again. At that moment, I can't recall the smoothness of her body or the moments of warmth that have never left my mind during my time away from her, those moments I'd make use of whenever Chris approached me in bed. I hold her in my arms once more and feel at that moment as if I've forgotten every memory that linked the two of us.

I listen to the rhythm of her calm, regular breathing and I know that she's surrendered to a short sleep, but before long it will be interrupted by nighttime pain. When we awake in the morning, I'm still embracing her, her body like an unborn child's.

Tomorrow we start chemotherapy, I tell her, and kiss her a morning kiss.

I wait for Nour but he doesn't come. I know that he's not in his office; I know that he's out somewhere. I've been waiting here for hours and his bedroom, which I've never liked, is lonely and cold. But I'll wait and I'll wait even longer because I know that if I walk out this door before seeing him I won't be able to return.

So I'll wait and this is how I'll pay back the debt of waiting that I owe him, because he waited for me so many times. It's as if the air in the room has decreased. Perhaps this explains my feeling of suffocation: if waiting for him in his flat where we first came together causes such feelings of suffocation, then love is useless. Should I just leave? Go back to Mombasa to see the man I don't want? Or wait for this other man who doesn't come? I postpone the moment of leaving. And so I delay every decision and every movement. I delay my whole life. In this way, I extend the period of my waiting ever more. I write and dilute my desire for him through writing. I make it dissipate and I forget. I look at the clock on my phone, which is lying next to me on the bed. It would have been better if I hadn't taken off my clothes. My nakedness is lonely; I can't bear it. Naked in a room that seems naked, with the whole world outside. I'm alone, waiting for him. I don't know why just then I remember what Georges said to me in his warm, seemingly hopeless voice when we spoke on the phone the night I left for Australia: "The most beautiful thing about you is that you have a strong presence, you're not controlled and you're soft, you're present and tender, very present and very gentle, you're strong and resilient. You give without weakness. This is what's unique to you: you don't allow a man to decode you too easily." Did he say everything that he thought about me all at once because he sensed that we'd never see each other again? Only now do I write down what Georges said. But I'm thinking only of Nour, who seems more and more mysterious as I grow closer to him. Every time I know his body more profoundly, I grow lonelier. I miss the smell of his skin…

Nour can't bear to stay in one place for long. Maybe the idea of searching for his roots was born out of this constant movement, so that he could travel. But his continual searching worries me, as does his being away. He's searching for his roots and believes that he's holding onto something, but in reality he's only holding onto shadows of the past, his illusions. "I don't belong here," he tells me, "I want to go back to my country." But does anyone have a "home" country? Don't we invent our own homelands? Perhaps Chris is right when he says that we don't need that many reasons to love a place and call it our homeland.

Nour returns to search for his roots. When he doesn't find them, he decides to leave. As for me, I see myself lost deeper and deeper in a spiral of waiting. It's OK, I tell myself. I'll learn how to leave once again, how to depart peacefully. Peacefully? This is the right word now. Peace inside me, in the walls of my womb, which trembles like a leaf whenever I think of him. There's an entire life that I have almost no power over and that's nourished by love.

The last time we met, I went into his apartment. I didn't see him and I didn't see his suitcase but I felt it. I knew that he must be in the bedroom. I pulled back the curtain and through the window I saw him sitting on the balcony, which isn't even wide enough for two people. He put on his sunglasses and tried over and over again to light his pipe. He looked at me from behind his sunglasses. I smiled at his repeated, failed attempts to light his pipe. He wanted to read on my face the impact he makes on me. He wanted to read the impact his coldness and appearance have on my eyes and body. He walked toward me and lifted his glasses from his eyes. I have missed his eyes. I miss the worry with which they sear me whenever I look into them. I know that I still need him more than he needs me. I know he has built a relationship with me within certain boundaries around his life, his work, his relationship to this place, women, his return to his homeland, and his search for his roots. He has chosen a place for me and kept me in this limited, narrow space.

Here I am, waiting once again. Another wait and another. The end of my last wait is still in my mind. For two weeks I wait for him in the café. I wait for some correspondence from him telling me that he's returned to Beirut, that the room is waiting for me and that he too waits for me. He says that he'll come back after two days and he doesn't come back. I wait an hour for him in the café, two hours, three. I wait for him even longer than this.

Wimpy fills up, Wimpy empties. Alone on my chair near the cold pane of glass, I look like a mannequin forgotten in a shop window. Our date was set for eight-thirty, time passes, it's ten o'clock and he still hasn't called. The waiter hovers around me. At ten o'clock I'm the last customer. The cafés and restaurants in Solidère are just getting started at ten, but here on this street, Hamra Street, it's closing time.

Across from me, Modca has transformed into *Veromoda*, with a big sign for *Jack & Jones*. I think, what if I pick up the orange and white chair I'm sitting on in Wimpy's sidewalk section, bring it over to the closed *Veromoda*, and sit there right in front of its door? It would seem unnatural to anyone who saw me there. People used to sit there but now people only walk in or look at the displays in the windows as they pass. Now it would be strange to put a chair on the sidewalk in front of it. No one sits in front of fancy boutiques except the man who takes bags from people as they enter, bags they've brought from other shops. He takes them to be sure no one puts anything from this shop in their bag when the owner's not looking.

Why I am here? I ask myself. Why hasn't he come yet? Why isn't my phone ringing? I put the ringer on very low so that only I can hear it. No doubt people know that I've been waiting three hours for him, that I asked for juice and then tea and then coffee and a grilled cheese sandwich. I also asked for a pack of cigarettes, Gitanes Lights.

The waiter tells me that they only have Marlboro and Marlboro Lights, so I take the Lights. I smoke thirteen cigarettes and stop. I keep the last seven cigarettes for when I go back to my apartment on Makhoul Street, for fear of running out once I'm home.

What will I do when I go back? I'll get in the bathtub and fill it with hot water. I'll take off the clothes that I spent hours choosing and changing. I left all the clothes that I'd taken out of the closet lying on my bed when I went out. It'll take some time to hang them all up again. But I feel incredibly sleepy and I won't do anything tonight. I can't do anything now except wait. The writing of waiting. The worry of waiting. The silence of waiting.

When will this nightmare of mine end? When will I be done dealing with the bureaucracy around our building and be free to go back? They told me by fax that it wouldn't take more than a month to finish everything. I've been here nine months and I'm still waiting.

I wake up because of a sound that I forget the moment I awake. I don't know what it is, but I'm sure that a sound woke me, though I always put little pieces of wax in my ears to block out the sounds of the world. They wake me up anyway. I sit up in bed, I try to put my feet down and get out of bed. I can't. I lie down, turn over onto my side, and look at the clock on my phone, which sits on my bedside table. It's seven AM and there are two *missed calls*. I look up the numbers. One is from Chris, at one o'clock in the morning, and the other is from Nour, at four o'clock in the morning. Bad timing! Yesterday, I didn't get even one call from Nour apologizing for standing me up and now I see that he tried to call me at four AM. Did he think

I would wait for him all night?
I try to get out of bed but I'm too weak; I try again and
I can't. Perhaps now I'm paralyzed.
   "I have nothing to give you except my love," I told
him the last time we met. He told me that this was too
much for him to handle and that perhaps I was unlucky
to have met him.
   I think that I'm a little bit lucky, but I don't answer.

He comes back to me three weeks later... We have
lunch together, then he says goodbye because he wants to
go to his office and read his email. I wait for him for two
weeks. He says that he'll be away for only one week, but
his trip lasts a whole eternity. When he comes back, I
don't want to say anything; I don't want to lay any blame.
I want only one thing: to be naked and let our bodies talk
to each other. This doesn't happen. He is tired and sleepy;
I've already started to calm down and my love is calm and
well-mannered. When I leave him, I'm not angry, only
sad, a slight pain gnawing at my soul.
   I go back to my flat to shower, to wash the traces of
defeat and distress from my body. A mere half-hour later
there's a knock on my apartment door. I know it's him;
I'm still in the shower. I get out, soap on my face and my
hair and body wet. I open the door to him and walk back
to the bathroom. He takes off his clothes and follows me.
He gets in the shower with me and embraces me... This
wet union tastes like heaven.
   There's something dramatic in his eyes when he
enters my body. I look at him and he closes his eyes,

embarrassed. I ask him to open his eyes and look at me, to look at my face and my full body underneath him; my body undulates under his body and eyes and desire. A slow movement from me and he slows his pleasure. His body receives mine, slowing its rhythmic motions. He waits for my body's rhythms to intensify and focus for one concentrated moment. Then he'll know I've reached my climax. He'll know this by watching the muscles on my face relax, the rhythm of my movements will slow and stop, my voice will lower, my breathing will slow. He says that he knows from the light in my eyes and the color of my skin. He says my skin takes on a shade he can't describe. He can only feel it.

We sit in the café that has become part of our relationship. He says that he'll go back to America the following week. The people we love stay with us, inside us until we're able to accept that we've lost them. But he can't stay with me until then, until he can deal with such loss. Every time his body enters mine, I live out my worry about saying goodbye. "I want you to stay." I say it and am afraid. I'm expecting fear, the fear of losing him. Then I add, "I know that life will go on if you return to America. I want you to stay here, it's true. But don't expect me to fight for you to stay." I protect myself with these words, but I'm lying. He leaves me and walks away. I stay on the chair in the café, alone. The coffee is cold and I start to cry.

I came looking for a man I didn't find. I've left another behind me, like someone who's gone on a long journey and only remembers this when she returns. I remember the journey but I'm not the same woman I was.

I can't be the woman I was because this journey isn't simply a memory and that's it—it is another life.

Nour comes to take me to the South to spend our last weekend together in the Orange House, a small family hotel run by two women. It took me a long time to leave my flat; I had to pack my suitcase. I forgot to do it when I woke up. He's waiting for me in his car in front of the building. From a distance, his eyes seem like those of someone who's about to lose hope. When I approach him I feel something new and different. As though I've finally accepted his trip to America. I tell myself that this time he's waiting for me. As though the act of waiting renews itself every day no matter which of us is waiting.

Love is amazing, but it doesn't change a person. This strikes me as we walk on the sandy seashore in front of the Orange House, the high waves crashing against the cement walls, their mist reaching my face and neck.

"Love is amazing," he reiterates, smiling, unconvinced of what he just said. Love is amazing but it doesn't change a person, I reply silently. You took a risk on love and lost, I tell myself.

I'm on the verge of saying just one thing to him: Save what we lived together. I say it in a low, barely audible, voice. I say it and my eyes expect nothing. Perhaps I say it only in order to keep a thin thread suspended between us. I know that he's not listening to me and won't be able to do anything for us. And I know that he's not searching for his roots but for a mere stitch of salvation. I don't say anything. I think about Nahil and what she said to Olga in the final days before she died, "There are things that are unspoken, simple and whole, like eyes."

Powerful waves crash high on the shore where we walk and spray their moisture on my hair and face. My lips are filled with the taste of salt. I open my body to the wave and its salt.

When we leave we die a little death. We die in peace. And we leave in peace. Parting is not simply a little death, it's returning to the selves that we'd forgotten in the exuberance of passion.

I wake up early and go down to walk on the beach alone. I want to swim right out into the deep water, where perhaps I can forget the feeling of heaviness that I've had since yesterday. I think about what Nour said to me the night before: he wants to travel, to go back to America, to settle his accounts with what's left of his emotions. I ask myself if what he's feeling are the leftovers of emotions from which he can't find relief.

Leftovers of emotions!

Did he return to Lebanon only to let go of them?

It's hard to swim in the sea by the Orange House because there are so many rocks scattered in the water. But I want to swim. And I want to see the sea turtles that find shelter and sanctuary for their young on this beach. I walk into the water and find it difficult to keep my balance. I try to swim but a powerful wave pushes me toward the rocks. My body crashes into them and I injure my leg. A second and a third wave take me. I return once again to the deeper water but another powerful wave propels me into other rocks. I try to swim free but I can't. I try very hard to relax and leave my body neutral, as I learned to do in my yoga classes. I emerge from the water with bruises on my legs and arms, all over my body. I sit on the sand and for a few moments feel like I can't walk. I try to stand up and I manage to, despite my pain.

I go back to the room and find Nour still sleeping. I go into the bathroom and wash the salt off my body, my bruises growing redder.

My swollen legs and arms pain me. I look at my body in the giant mirror that covers an entire wall of the bathroom and in the image reflected back I see that I've started to look like someone who can fit in better in Beirut.

I put on a loose, flowing, long-sleeved shirt. I leave a little note for Nour and go out to a nearby café to have breakfast, ignoring my injuries. No time passes before he comes and sits down across from me; he brings his body close, right to the edge of the table that brings us together. He seems to be putting all his weight on the table, as if he wants to get rid of it, to eliminate the small space that separates our two bodies. He says that in Lebanon his dreams have faltered, that he was more optimistic before he came. He says that he lives a strange life, that there's a mere thread between himself and madness, a thread that he imagines might break at any moment, except that luck's been on his side. He lifts his coffee cup, drinks a little and then adds, "Or perhaps it's my bad luck that this thread hasn't broken." It's as if he's apologizing, though I don't know for what. I contemplate the gray hair that frames his face; he seems like a young man whose head has been invaded by gray too soon.

There's a message from Olga on the screen of my phone. I read the words "be happy." Be happy, I repeat bitterly. It's not until that moment that I tell myself that I won't return to Mombasa, I won't go back to Chris.

I look up from the screen and find Nour toying with the cigarette butts in the ashtray. He's daydreaming, sad.

I sleep most of the way back to Beirut from the South. Nour drives silently and doesn't want to talk.

He calls me in the early evening, at the very moment I return to Beirut with Olga. I haven't seen him for five days. I've been going to the hospital with Olga for her chemotherapy. I'm tired and don't answer his call. He sends me a short text, asking me to meet him one last time. The next morning he'll fly to Chicago.

I text him back, "*Have a nice trip back home!*"

Translator's Note

Like so many translators of creative literature, I am rarely satisfied with my work. So my initial experience of rendering Iman Humaydan's third novel, *Other Lives*, in English came as somewhat of a surprise. When I first started working, words came to me more easily than they have in the past. Over long sessions I felt as if the ideas and aesthetic properties of the text were merging together into a readable English. At a certain point, I felt that this novel would perhaps not simply be the easiest I have translated, but the best work I had ever produced.

But this confidence and feeling of ease did not last long. The process of reworking the translation from the draft produced by these first attempts into a final form was as painfully difficult as translation can be. I spent hours looking at specific passages, and even specific words, convinced that I had not conveyed either the ideas or the emotions of the text in Arabic. I could not possibly show what I had produced to Iman, let alone send it to the publisher. Despite my years of experience, I was surprised at both my initial feeling of confidence and my subsequent feeling that it would be impossible to translate this work.

Why was transforming *Hayawat Okhra* into *Other Lives* so easy and so difficult? I have used this question to structure some reflections on the process of translating this novel.

The idea of "intimacy with the text," as invoked by some scholars of translation, has helped me think through my own translation process for *Other Lives*. Developed in some depth by Gayatri Spivak in her well-known article "The Politics of Translation," the idea is that translators— particularly white women translating texts from the so-called third world—must have a deep knowledge of not only the texts they are working with, but the source and target languages and literary cultures. Intimacy here means knowing more than just what the words "mean," but also calling upon the layers of meaning words create within readers and reading cultures on both sides of the translation's linguistic divide.

In a series of "Rules for Translation" that I produced for the popular blog *Arabic Literature (in English)*, I put this simply: (1) Choose a text you love and (2) Respect the text. But these prescriptive statements are much easier to make than they are to either quantify or fulfill. Indeed, I do love *Hayawat Okhra* for many reasons and I have endeavored to respect it while changing it into *Other Lives*. But claiming an intimacy with the text, as a white, non-Arab translator, is a more complex proposition. Part of what gave me a sense of closeness with the book was my deep awareness that even as I related to it I was inevitably distant from it as well.

First and foremost, I am not Lebanese; I did not live in Lebanon during the civil war. While the kinds of questions and issues so central to *Other Lives* are familiar to me and essential to many people I know—particularly the question of being permitted to forget or forced to remember—they are not central to my own life. I do not have the long history with Lebanon, the close family ties and proximity to the terrible violence of the war that Myriam and the other characters experience.

But when I think about "intimacy with the text," I must also consider how my close friendship and comradeship with Iman Humaydan provides a unique advantage in translating her work. Because she and I have talked extensively and share certain bonds, I can at times get inside the language of the text in ways that I would not have be able to without her. My understanding of the depths of her creative work owes a great deal to this connection and to her generosity in spending the time to work and think together about language and the issues that underlie her writing.

I also translated Iman's second novel, *Toot barri*, as *Wild Mulberries* (Interlink, 2008), which offered me a familiarity with her style and themes, as well as an established working relationship. This fact also presented me with a challenge, to keep the works somewhat consistent in style and approach—to create a voice for Iman in English. This is something that I have advocated for in my academic writing on translation politics, but which I have not had the opportunity to do previously. Translating two novels by the same author gave me a privileged position inside the text and author's worlds. I am aware that claiming a bond with the original writer of the novel means that I am claiming that she "authorizes" my translation and this gives it weight. But I know that I am still very much an outsider to the text, language and world that Myriam and the other characters inhabit in *Other Lives*. Some intimacies are forged through such connections but other gaps can never be bridged—despite whatever respect and good intentions a translator has.

Precisely the thing that is meant to make a translation "better"—this elusive intimacy with the text—at different points threatened to stall the entire project. An example of this is the hauntingly tragic scene of the death of Myriam's brother Baha'. The violence that Myriam witnessed and experienced affected her body. She had nightmares and often felt suffocated. As I was working on these sections—particularly the descriptions of Myriam's nightmares about trees—I could often experience Myriam's sense of suffocation. The experience felt real to me. It seemed impossible to try to convey, in translation, the emotion of passages that had such a deep impact on me as a reader.

The first time I read the novel, I did not experience this same visceral reaction. In fact, the passages that affected me the most upon the first reading were those about Myriam's reactions to Olga's cancer, her contemplation of their long friendship and the way she supported her friend at the end of her life. My reaction to the passages about Olga's cancer seemed "natural" to me, as it is close to my own embodied experience—I was undergoing cancer treatments myself while translating the book. Textual intimacy is a concept often invoked and difficult to define, as is how it is connected to embodied experience. Perhaps what makes Iman's writing so powerful is how deeply it touches and exposes human experiences, particularly those that we often do not speak—most particularly, the lives of women marked by violence. We see Myriam as a woman who often feels disconnected from the people around her and the places she inhabits. She is restlessly in motion, searching for a home she cannot find. Her inability to settle is meticulously laid bare and depicted in all its raw emotions. Iman gives readers a privileged insight into Myriam's psyche, the places inside Myriam where her unspoken emotions can be expressed.

This concept of textual intimacy, however, offers little practical insight into the specifics of the translation process. In this translation I have used a number of techniques that are based on the principle of allowing the text to "read as a translation," in order to capture the beauty and haunting qualities of the Arabic original. I have worked closely with the editor of this work, Hilary Plum, to create a balance in the novel between a smooth or easily readable text and a text that continually reminds the reader that it was not originally written in English. For example, the words that appear in italics in the translation are all written in Latin letters in English in the original novel. Preserving the italics gives the reader a sense of the layering of language in the original.

In rendering this work in English, I also had to face the challenge of *Hayawat Okhra*'s mix of narrative styles. The novel unfolds through both deeply personal, excruciatingly and intensely depicted passages and dry, factual, almost disconnected narrative passages. To reproduce this in English is difficult. The short declarative sentences written in deceptively simple Arabic work differently than such sentences might in English, where they may sound inconsistent or boring. I did not wish to sacrifice this aspect's of the work's narrative technique for the sake of making the translation smoother or more—as the translation theorists say—"domesticated."

Another challenge specific to this novel was how to represent references to the Druze community, particularly implicit references, with which many readers presumably would not be familiar. I decided that my overarching goal was to preserve the aesthetic qualities of the novel, so I chose not to include a glossary or to "cushion" passages with explanations not available in the original. Some of this sort of cushioning exists in the Arabic novel; the author explains such things as the transmigration of souls and how this belief circulates amongst Druze characters. But I have not added additional references. The most important example is the layered meanings of the title *Hayawat Okhra*, and its use of a relatively esoteric Arabic plural of the word for life, which can imply a Druze understanding of "lives." The English title, *Other Lives*, cannot convey these layers of meaning.

All translation from Arabic into English faces the challenge of how to translate tenses. The most important translation strategy I used in *Other Lives* was to render much of the novel's narration in the present tense. This novel moves back and forth between times and places so seamlessly that the confusion of tenses adds to the text's meaning rather than detracts from it. Motion, Myriam's physical and spiritual restlessness, is a major theme of the work. Because Myriam herself confesses that she experiences time as nonlinear—she describes time as a spiral—I have conveyed as much of the text's main narration as possible in the present tense; this means that some of what is written about in the present tense here happened "in the past." Creating this confusion and questioning about time within the narration itself challenges the reader constantly to be aware of the importance of space, time and chronology in the novel. This very much mirrors my own challenges as a translator who has sought to give "other lives" to this novel by transforming it into English.

Michelle Hartman, Montréal, January 2014

Translator's Acknowledgments

First and most importantly, I would like to acknowledge Iman Humaydan's participation in and contributions to this translation, not only as the work's author but also as a colleague and friend. Working with Iman has been a true collaboration; I have learned so much in the process of talking about language and literature together and for this I am extremely grateful.

For a number of reasons, this translation took some time to appear in print. Thanks to the people at Interlink for making it happen and to Michel Moushabeck for his patience. Much more than a line of thanks is due to Hilary Plum. It is not a cliché to say that her work is truly more than that of an editor, even a really good one. Her careful and thorough eye, together with a love of and flair for literature in translation has made this translation as good as it is. The bulk of this translation was finished in Lebanon and I would like to extend the warmest possible thanks to Yasmine Nachabe and all the Taans for providing me with space and conversations that greatly improved the work. Much of it was completed in Yasmine's office at the Lebanese American University and she, along with other friends and colleagues at LAU, offered me the opportunity to teach translation theory and politics while working on it. Merci kteer to Elise Salem, Mariam Marroum and Nada Saab. I would also like to acknowledge the participants in my 2011 LAU seminar on translation: Zeina al-Abed, Eylaf Badreddine, Hicham Kharroub, Mona Majzoub and Yasmine Nachabe. Shukran to Abbas Beydoun for helping facilitate the opportunity to talk about this translation with Iman in Sour. Students at McGill also contributed to this translation—thanks in particular to Dima Ayoub and Shirin Radjavi, as well as Katy Kalemkerian, for helping it take its final shape. Rula Jurdi Abisaab and Malek Abisaab provided conversation and support that helped me to complete the translation, as did Aziz Choudry and rosalind hampton. As always, I must acknowledge the women whose work allowed me to complete this work. Thanks in particular to my mother Julia, sister Amanda, (Mama) Rachel, Alison, Marie, Amar, Randa and Farah.

This book follows Myriam's trajectory from Beirut to Adelaide to Mombasa and back to Beirut, tracing her path as she searches for a way to fit into this world and find home. A life journey that encompasses Sialkot–South London–Christchurch–Montreal is different but shares many similarities; I dedicate this translation to someone who has trod that path and to others on their own journeys to find home.